WELCOME
RESTART ME UP
THE UNAUTHORIZED, UN-ACCURATE ORAL HISTORY OF WINDOWS 95
WRITTEN BY
LESLEY TSINA

THE DEVASTATOR

Written by
Lesley Tsina

Contributing Editors
Patrick Baker
Asterios Kokkinos

Editors
Geoffrey Golden
Amanda Meadows

Cover Design
Spencer Dina

First Edition: August 2015
Second Edition: October 2016
2.5 Edition: January 2020

devastatorpress.com

PRINTED IN THE ~~BACK OF AN APPLE STORE~~ USA

To Dad, who once told me several billion email-forwarded Windows 95 jokes while I was trying to eat breakfast. I hope these jokes are funnier.

And to the Internet, which, ironically, made this book possible.

END-READER LICENSE AGREEMENT FOR RESTART ME UP

IMPORTANT—READ SLOWLY AND VERY, VERY CAREFULLY: This End-Reader License Agreement ("ERLA") is a surprisingly legal agreement between you (the "Reader") and The Devastator (aka "Cool Dudez Inc.") or any of its affiliates ("Cool Chickz Ltd."). YOU AGREE TO BE BOUND BY THE TERMS OF THIS ERLA BY READING, BROWSING, TOUCHING, SMOKING OR OTHERWISE USING THIS BOOK. IF YOU DO NOT AGREE, DO NOT READ, TALK ABOUT, QUOTE, GLANCE AT, SNORT OR ADORABLY GIGGLE AT THIS BOOK.

1. RIGHTS OF READER. Cool Dudez Inc. (aka "The Devastator") grants you the right to read this here book if you comply with the terms and conditions of this ERLA:

1.1 Satire. You agree that Restart Me Up is a work of satire, which grants this book protection under the Fair Use Act. You also acknowledge that many great American cultural institutions have received protection under this act, such as *Hustler Magazine* and 2 Live Crew.

1.2 Fiction. You agree that this book is a work of fiction. Any similarities between living persons and characters in this book are entirely coincidental. Real product and company names were used without permission for literary effect. In summary, this book is completely made up. The author even took made up portions and further fictionalized them.

1.3 No Lawsuits! You agree not to sue the author, The Devastator, Cool Dudes Inc., Cool Chickz Ltd., Party Bros. Entertainment, or any of its affiliates. You agree not to send The Devastator any "Cease and Desist" communications or threats of legal action. No creepy midnight phone calls, pervert. You agree that everything we're doing here is so legal that it deserves a standing ovation. Also, don't sue us. We have no money!

1.4 Auto Root Update. The Auto Root Update feature is… uh, something. We don't know. Maybe you should switch it off? It sounds like a painful dental procedure.

● I ACCEPT THIS AGREEMENT.
○ THERE IS NO OTHER OPTION.

NEXT >

TABLE OF CONTENTS

FOREWORD

Everyone has a Windows 95 story. From the guy who camped out at CompUSA to buy it, to the engineer who blames it for his divorce. These stories echo across the globe, from the halls of the Microsoft campus to the armchair section of your local Starbucks.

As we approach the twentieth anniversary of Windows 95, it seemed only fitting to collect these memories into a massive volume of tribute. Our team of interviewers snuck into press junkets, lurked on message boards and talked their way onto private islands to find interview subjects. We were threatened, flamed, and in one case, shot with a crossbow. After transcribing and editing hundreds of .WAV files, we produced our initial 5000-page manuscript. Then the lawyers took their pass and we ended up with the slim volume you now hold in your hand.

This is the story of Windows 95, as told by the people who were there: from ordinary citizens to Bill Gates himself. No single book can encompass every detail of such a monumental achievement. But I hope that our work stands as a testament to the creators, the testers, the customers, the marketers, the weirdos, and that one giant bug. To hype yet unmatched in this century. To software that has stood the test of time.

To Windows 95!

Lesley Tsina

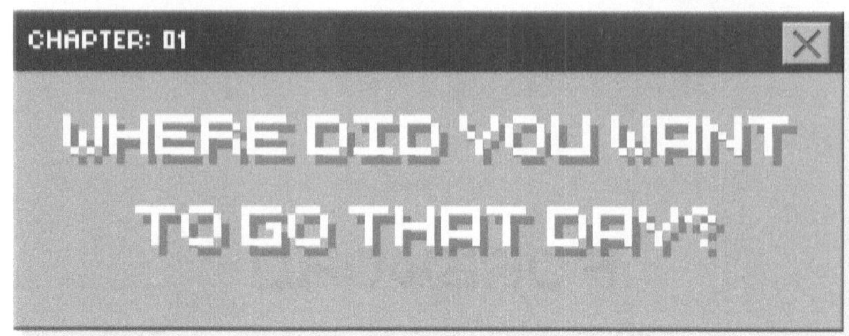

Every schoolchild knows that August 24th, 1995 was the launch of Windows 95. We began our journey by asking every single person in line at the Redmond, Washington Starbucks where they were on 8/24.

KELLY SIMMS, *Administrative Assistant*:
It was an ordinary day. I made breakfast, fed the cat, drove to work. I was just pulling into the parking lot when they mentioned it on the radio. And I took the rest of the day off.

MATT KLINMAN, *Accountant*:
I was tired. I'd been up all night waiting for the stroke of midnight, counting and recounting the change in my piggy bank to make sure I had $89. Between my birthday money, my salary from Baskin Robbins, and my allowance, I had just enough. It was like Christmas, only I was buying myself the best present in the world: a consumer-oriented upgrade to the Windows 3.1 operating system. I biked down to the store right after school.

SAMANTHA TRACE, *Former Child*:
I remember my dad came home that night with a package under his arm, and we all gathered around. And he said, "This is going to change our lives."

TYRONE WILLIAMS, *Sales Executive*:
I was flying home from Paris on business, and I saw the Microsoft logo on the fields of Southern France. They must have painted it. I was so jazzed, I bought it at the airport when I landed.

RUSSELL DENNIS, *Software Engineer*:
I was doing really badly in school. Getting into fights, vandalism, stuff like that. Then, my math teacher took us to the movie theater to watch a satellite broadcast of the launch. I was overwhelmed by the sheer glamour of it. And I decided to become a software engineer.

EMILY DORFMAN, *College Professor*:
It was all over the news. I opened the paper and there was a full page spread. It was everywhere.

MANNY PASTERNAK, *Tech Support Specialist*:
When I got it home I just stared at the box before I even opened it. That night, I slept with the manual on my pillow. My girlfriend had just left me.

EVAN VALDEZ, *Software Engineer*:
I was working at Apple. We were like, *nice try, assholes.*

MICKI DAVIDSON, *Windows Groupie*:
My girlfriend and I were sophomores at Reed, and we drove up from Portland to try and sneak into the launch party. We got a guy downtown to make us fake Microsoft IDs. We were crazy!

Make_It_S0, *Usenet Nerd*:
I slept through it because I'd been up watching episodes of Voyager on VHS. I felt like such an asshole because the Brian Eno message board was blowing up when I logged on.

BRIAN DANIELSON, *Tech Blogger*:
It's been 20 years? God, I'm old.

LANCE JACKSON, *Windows 95 Engineer*:
We all woke up that morning and thought, *this is it.* It's all on the line. We succeed, or we crash and burn. But even so, we'd been in a bubble for 18 months. We had no idea how big this thing was going to be. We put on our polos and Dockers and vanpooled to campus. I cannot adequately describe the level of tension and expectation. To really know what the stakes were, you had to have been on the project. It's a hell of a story. How much time do you have? ✕

The Microsoft campus in Redmond, Washington. A verdant corporate wonderland, populated by the brilliant, the competitive, and the eccentric. We visited the campus, looking for Windows 95's origin stories. Who are the people who brought Windows 95 to life? We sat outside Building 2, watching giant koi swim in the man-made pond employees call "Lake Bill." There, we listened to dozens of people's memories of the project. We were surprised to find that many of the key players had one thing in common: a vanpool.

LANCE JACKSON, *Software Engineer:*
The vanpool was my idea. I was living in Seattle and had to get to Redmond every day. It was more efficient to do a rideshare. So I hand-picked the most compatible developers within easy driving distance of my apartment. We called ourselves the Vanpool 8. Because we were officially Vanpool 8. And there were eight of us.

BRIANNA LEE, *Software Development Manager:*
It was Lance's vanpool, and he invited a bunch of us. Lance is a good guy. Although he does talk a lot. I went on a date with him once and he spent the whole time explaining the history of the banana.

LANCE JACKSON:
The development of the modern banana is really quite surprising. How much time do you have?

STAN BANAS, *Software Engineer:*
Lance Jackson never shuts up. He thinks everything is so goddamn interesting. It's like a Russian novel. He'll go to the coffee room and then recap, in excruciating detail, his trip to the coffee room. And his philosophy on coffee. And rooms.

BRIANNA LEE:
Stan Banas is an asshole. The only reason he was in the vanpool is that he had a condo in the same building as Lance and he whined his way in.

STAN BANAS:
Brianna Lee went to Harvard. That's her entire personality in a nutshell. Bill Gates dropped out of Harvard. She is no Bill Gates.

BRIANNA LEE:
I went to Harvard. Deal with it.

STAN BANAS:
Then there was Vlad. His full name is Vlad Michael Murray, which wasn't funny at the time. He was a lifer, Microsoft straight out of college. Not the smartest guy, kind of a workhorse. I'd say on a scale of 1 to Bill Gates, he's a soft 6. I'm a 12.5.

VLAD MICHAEL MURRAY, *Software Engineer:*
Yeah, I don't rank very high on Stan's made up intelligence scale. The highest anyone ever got was an 8.9. Except for Bill, of course.

LANCE JACKSON:
Vlad is not stupid. He just feigns narcolepsy whenever Stan Banas is around. Narcolepsy is a fascinating disorder…

BRIANNA LEE:
There was Kanwar, the guy who sang all the time. He was super into the Microsoft Choir.

KANWAR KHAN, *Software Engineer:*
(singing) *Bill Gates is a mighty god and a mighty ruler / over all false idols.* It's based on a Mendelssohn hymn.

VLAD MICHAEL MURRAY:
Those choir guys were intense. They sang songs in assembly language.

KANWAR KHAN:
It's very complicated. They actually used our songs to screen new developers.

JOSH COOPER, *Software Engineer:*
I remember they handed me a page of sheet music during my technical interview and told me to translate it and find errors. It was a song called "Morning Has Broken Over Building 8, Let Us Now Debug."

KANWAR KHAN:
Josh was a new hire, he came on right before Win95. We were afraid of Josh. We called him the Oracle of Coding. I mean, he isn't a real oracle. The only genuine oracle is at Oracle. Larry Ellison has her under lock and key.

STAN BANAS:
Josh is a 9.9.

JOSH COOPER:
Stan Banas is a tool.

KANWAR KHAN:
Josh was the one who made Stan Banas stop hogging shotgun.

STAN BANAS:
I called shotgun for two years. I'm just that fast. But then Josh came in and suddenly there was a goddamn weekly rotation.

BRIANNA LEE:
We let him have shotgun because he would call it the second we turned the corner in the parking lot. It was pathetic. And then Josh came along and said, "Why don't you guys just rotate?" And we were scared of him, so we did. It was awesome.

VLAD MICHAEL MURRAY:
Calvin didn't talk much. He always had headphones on. I heard he was running a major Shadowrun campaign over in Building 7, but he never talked about that either.

CALVIN VASQUEZ, *Software Engineer:*
Yes.

LANCE JACKSON:
Lisa K. had a dog.

STAN BANAS:
Lisa K. was just kind of boring.

BRIANNA LEE:
Lisa K. Yeah.

LISA [KNUDSEN], *Software Engineer:*
Why does everyone still call me Lisa K.? There are no other Lisas at
Microsoft. There was a Lisa who retired like, 3 years before I started.
Just call me Lisa Knudsen. Or Lisa.

VLAD MICHAEL MURRAY:
God, we spent a lot of time in that van. Feels like my whole life was
van, work, Denny's, van, sleep. Good times.

LANCE JACKSON:
I was very proud of my vanpool. Do you want to hear about the
history of vanpooling?

*Every piece of software starts with a problem. In this case, the problem was
small. Ish. Microsoft needed to upgrade Windows 3.1, its consumer-grade
operating system. The plan was to do some bug fixes, improve the clunky
parts of its graphical user interface, and release it as Windows 93. That
turned out to be a dumb idea and Windows 93 became a larger update,
codenamed Chicago. We asked our group why they joined the project.*

BRIANNA LEE:
I just wanted an office with a window. It is an open secret at Microsoft
that the way to get a window was to ship a version of Windows. When
they announced Chicago, I realized this was my chance.

LANCE JACKSON:
It's simple. Bill Gates is God. And you want God to love you, even
though you fear him. The best way to earn God's love is to work on
stuff he likes. Then, your devotion to God grants you a window to
the outside world.

KANWAR KHAN:
I think Lance grew up in some kind of weird church community. Not
sure. But yeah, everyone wanted a window.

VLAD MICHAEL MURRAY:
You would think that getting a window would be easier – all of the
buildings were shaped like Xs for maximum window office capacity.
But that also meant that if you didn't have one it made you feel like
an even bigger loser. We were called "The Unwindowed."

JOSH COOPER:
I heard about the window thing. I was new and Unwindowed. I figured, might be bullshit, but it's worth a shot.

BRIANNA LEE:
My office sucked. I was between a bathroom and an elevator.

VLAD MICHAEL MURRAY:
My office was haunted. If I had a window, the ghosts could escape.

LANCE JACKSON:
My girlfriend broke up with me, and becoming windowed was part of my eight-point plan to get her back.

KANWAR KHAN:
I wanted to be able to look up from my work and contemplate the beauty of nature. It feeds my creativity. Also, I'd been on the waiting list to get a window for a year and a half, which was bullshit.

STAN BANAS:
I already had a window. But Level 13s get a window that actually opens. And I wanted to be a Level 13.

VLAD MICHAEL MURRAY:
Ughhhh, of course Stan Banas was obsessed with his level.

LANCE JACKSON:
Everyone has a level. Josh, for example, is a Level 7, since he's just out of school. Level 1 is a sandwich artist in the cafeteria. No wait, apprentice sandwich artist. Level 13 is a big jump. It requires severe brown nosing, so I'm actually surprised Banas hadn't gotten it by then.

STAN BANAS:
When you reach Level 13 they increase your stock options. And you are allowed to wear swag from any project without ridicule. And you get a card that lets you get chips out of the vending machine for free.

BRIANNA LEE:
So to get on Windows, you had to go to Todd Bronstein. That guy was badass. He would ride his BMX to work. In January.

TODD BRONSTEIN, *VP, Microsoft Chicago:*
I'd worked on DOS 6.0, Windows 3.1, and in my spare time I was
learning classic BMX tricks. For me, it was a kind of meditation.
Whenever I got stuck on a problem, I'd go out into the courtyard and
do pogos and megaspins until I had an idea.

KANWAR KHAN:
He was pretty good. I was impressed that he could do that stuff
wearing khakis. When he was really stuck, he'd do it in front of
Building 8, where Bill could see him.

BILL GATES, *Former Chairman and CEO of Microsoft:*
I used to watch Todd from my office, hopping around on his bike.
It did seem to get him back on track. I say whatever works. Some
people juggle. Todd does wheelies.

KANWAR KHAN:
Then there were other days when he'd go out there all pissed off and
just keep grinding on ledges until security made him stop.

BILL GATES:
That was a dead giveaway. If he yelled at security, I knew Chicago's
schedule was slipping.

*Microsoft was also working on a more advanced project, a <boring>
completely new 32-bit operating system with an object-oriented shell and
file system and distributed computing features that promised "information
at your fingertips." </boring> The project was codenamed Cairo and was
said to be the future of Windows.*

BILL GATES:
All projects at Microsoft are given an internal codename. Windows
NT was Daytona, Microsoft Bob was Utopia, and Encarta was
Gandalf. For Windows, we were in the middle of a run of city
names. So our two OS projects were called Chicago and Cairo.
Because Chicago's a pretty good vacation, but Cairo would be
totally awesome.

TODD BRONSTEIN:
There wasn't just Chicago and Cairo, there were also several
Windows teams working on parallel versions that were abandoned
along the way. I remember Dayton, Quincy, Glendale, New Rochelle,
Tirana, and Svalbard.

BILL GATES:
Actually, we kept Svalbard going for a long time. In case of nuclear attack, we wanted to make sure there was an off-site development team at an undisclosed location. Which was actually in Svalbard, just to confuse people.

VLAD MICHAEL MURRAY:
There's a longstanding rumor that they never accounted for every developer on Windows at the end of the project. Some say they wander the ice bunker of Svalbard, awaiting Windows 95 to this very day...

TODD BRONSTEIN:
Yeah, no.

Microsoft Chicago and Microsoft Cairo were both being developed at the same time. This caused a certain amount of tension between teams.

LANCE JACKSON:
Oh man, those guys on Cairo were so irritating. They all rollerbladed to work together. They acted like it was some kind of big deal but really, most of it was downhill.

STAN BANAS:
They'd skate alongside our van and slap the windows. Smug bastards. Plus, they all had Ph.D.s which is totally, totally excessive. They were lamer than Lance Jackson.

LANCE JACKSON:
I'd tell you the history of rollerblading, but I don't want to give those jerks credit for being a part of something that cool.

LISA K.:
And Derek gave them whatever they wanted.

DEREK UNTERBERG, *VP, Microsoft Cairo:*
I like to make my team feel special. And they were. They were making the OS of the future, light years beyond Chicago. Word on the street was that the Chicago folks were bitter and Unwindowed. My team didn't need windows. They had imaginations.

BRIANNA LEE:
It was annoying. He made them Cairo swag before the project was even really going. Not cool. They had their own soda fridge, and it had exactly the same sodas as ours. Like for some reason their lips were too delicate for the sodas of the masses.

KANWAR KHAN:
All the sodas were free! Why would they lock theirs up?

VLAD MICHAEL MURRAY:
What really pissed me off was that Cairo had awesome computers. Whereas we had stupid Todd-boxes.

LISA K.:
Todd insisted that everyone on Chicago use outdated hardware so we could see how the OS would work in the wild. It made sense. But it just sucked.

LANCE JACKSON:
Oh God, Todd-boxes. Minesweeper ran slowly on these machines. It was torture. And then the Cairo guys has 486s. It wasn't fair. They got 21-inch monitors, too!

DEREK UNTERBERG:
We had the best of the best. Because we were the best of the best.

LANCE JACKSON:
They were the absolute worst.

JOSH COOPER:
I got offered a spot on Cairo, but I would've hated myself too much.

BRIANNA LEE:
Getting on Chicago was a calculated risk. We all knew they wouldn't keep both Chicago and Cairo, long term. Only one project would move forward after Bill's review. And Cairo was sexier.

TODD BRONSTEIN:
Sexy and mysterious. Like Derek, blading around Lake Bill on his lunch hour. He's very graceful. What a tool. ▨

Once the Chicago team was staffed, they started working on a prototype. We went to Microsoft's Usability Lab to talk about the design process.

TODD BRONSTEIN, *VP, Microsoft Chicago*:
The major complaints about Windows 3.1 were that it was not like the Mac and that it was hard to use. We said, "We know. Can you be more specific?" They said things like, "It's just, you know, hard," and "When is lunch?" We asked the usability group to look into this.

GAIL KELLY, *Lead Usability Engineer*:
People didn't understand the file system.

ROBERT CHAN, *Usability Engineer*:
People would say stuff like, "How can there be a folder inside of another folder?" We would show them with an actual paper folder and they'd say "but why?" and we'd say "it's better" and they'd say "how do you fit it into the drawer?" and we'd say "it's a fucking metaphor!" and then someone would usually stop the test and make me take a walk around the building.

DAVE CIACCIO, *Usability Engineer*:
Lots of people didn't understand how to find a program and start it. Which was bad news for our software sales teams.

GAIL KELLY:
People wouldn't know a program was still open if there was something else open on top of the window. So they'd just open the same program over and over and over again until they ran out of memory.

ROBERT CHAN:
Eventually we just stopped making it possible to open 20 copies of Word. But that was in like, 1998.

See Figure.01 (page 72) for a look at the Windows 3.1 desktop.

TODD BRONSTEIN:
Then we started testing prototypes of Chicago. You never really know what you have until you watch people use it. It's very informative.

DAVE CIACCIO:
It's the worst.

GAIL KELLY:
We'd put people in a room and ask them to think out loud while they used the prototype. Oh my God. People would say things like, "This engineer is very attractive. Hello Nurse!" And then we'd tell them to stop thinking out loud.

ROBERT CHAN:
We would ask them to complete a task, like finding a file or opening Word and we'd tell them there were no wrong answers. And then we'd go outside and punch something.

DAVE CIACCIO:
The thing that just killed me was that nobody understood double-clicking. We were like, *are Windows users just morons?* When I touch a book twice, it means I'm about to open it.

GAIL KELLY:
Dave has OCD.

ROBERT CHAN:
I had this idea that maybe the mouse could have two buttons and if you clicked the one on the right, you could open up other things. It would be called right-clicking. The users were like ARE YOU INSANE? DO I LOOK LIKE I HAVE A DEGREE IN COMPUTER SCIENCE?

GAIL KELLY:
It was even worse when they started making suggestions. Like, "Can you make it more cyberpunk?" Or "Can we have pizza today for lunch?" Most of them we threw out because they were just stupid.

ROBERT CHAN:
Someone asked if we could make it easier to get onto the World Wide
Web. We basically told him to go fuck himself.

TODD BRONSTEIN:
Oh, hindsight...

*After many iterations and user tests, the basic features of Windows 95 began
to emerge. A surprising number of features were inspired by Todd Bronstein's
software muse. Otherwise known as his mom.*

STAN BANAS, *Software Engineer:*
Todd Bronstein was weirdly into his mom.

VLAD MICHAEL MURRAY, *Software Engineer:*
Yeah, what is it with that guy and his mom?

TODD BRONSTEIN:
All I said was that this software should be so easy to use that my mom
could use it. She's an ordinary user.

KANWAR KHAN, *Software Engineer:*
He moved her into the office! He moved her into *my* office!

ARLENE BRONSTEIN, *Todd's Mom:*
Todd asked me if I could come in to work with him on The Windows. I
got a computer and everything. I had solitaire, even.

BRIANNA LEE, *Software Development Manager:*
I think when she started writing the spec it got out of hand. She had
veto powers. It was nuts.

STAN BANAS:
What's worse is that Gates loved her. Arlene was untouchable.

BILL GATES, *Former Chairman and CEO of Microsoft:*
Arlene. What a woman. What a delight.

ARLENE BRONSTEIN:
I just made a few suggestions, here and there. Todd's sister Roz
had just visited me and she got me an Apple Mac. I liked it a lot.
It was cute.

TODD BRONSTEIN:
Do not get me started on Roz.

ARLENE BRONSTEIN:
I said to Todd, "Maybe it should be more like the Apple Mac." I
showed them.

KANWAR KHAN:
She brought a Mac Classic into *my* office!

LANCE JACKSON, *Software Engineer:*
A traitor in our midst.

ARLENE BRONSTEIN:
I said, "Maybe the Windows should have a little trash can, like the
Apple Mac."

TODD BRONSTEIN:
And the Recycle Bin was born.

See Figure.02 (page 73) to see the evolution of the Recycle Bin.

*The Chicago team added even bigger changes to the Graphical User Interface
(GUI). They developed the Start button, the Taskbar and Windows Explorer.*

STAN BANAS:
We decided we needed to have just one big button on the screen
that said "Start" that was for starting stuff. Because face it, people
are stupid.

TODD BRONSTEIN:
We decided that, like the Mac, we would call the home screen the
desktop. But we were going to be innovative and put all the buttons
and commands on the bottom.

BRIANNA LEE:
And every open file or program would also have a little bar on the
bottom of the screen so you wouldn't have to remember what was
running and could switch between windows. We called that part of
the desktop the Taskbar.

LANCE JACKSON:
It was supposed to be like *Cheers*. Where all the little windows hung
out and you knew their names.

VLAD MICHAEL MURRAY:
We came up with that during the period when Todd was making us test the GUI drunk to simulate the skill level of the average user. That was fun. Until it wasn't.

BRIANNA LEE:
HR made him stop when Calvin threw up during his performance review.

CALVIN VASQUEZ, *Software Engineer*:
Yes.

See Figure.03 (page 74) and Figure.04 (page 75) for early versions of the Start button and the Taskbar.

KANWAR KHAN:
We made Windows Explorer, which was an easier way to navigate to different files and folders. I wrote a song about it for the Microsoft Chorus. It was called "I Once Explored a Window Fair…"

LISA K.:
Windows Explorer sounded cooler. Like you were going on a little journey of discovery, not just trying to figure out where the hell you put that erotic X-Files fanfic you were writing. Or…may have been writing.

Certain features were controversial.

GAIL KELLY:
Big problem: research told us that most users spent an average of 21 full days a year trying to install hardware on Windows 3.1. That's nearly a month.

DAVE CIACCIO:
Internally we called it "DOS-ember."

LANCE JACKSON:
Eventually they came up with Plug and Play. The idea was that the system would automatically detect and configure whatever hardware was connected to it.

JOSH COOPER, *Software Engineer:*
Originally, Plug and Play was so powerful that your machine would control whatever was plugged into the same surge protector. Like, it would control your blender. Nobody was able to explain it. The world wasn't ready for it. We had to dumb it down.

STAN BANAS:
Some say we dumbed it down until it was useless. I think we avoided a dystopian future.

TODD BRONSTEIN:
Another problem: everyone complained that it was too hard to install a printer. We had a dialogue box for that in 3.1, but nobody could get through it. We knew it was bad because the letters we got were handwritten.

GAIL KELLY:
So we came up with the idea of Wizards. They'd show you how to install a printer, like a wizard would.

TODD BRONSTEIN:
Most of the developers felt like the term "wizard" was too strong.

KANWAR KHAN:
There was a lot of internal debate over whether or not a wizard would bother to help you install a printer. It's like getting three wishes and asking the genie to put your duvet cover on. It's a waste of magic.

LANCE JACKSON:
It also basically assumes that you'd *need* a fucking wizard to do half of the things that should be easy to do on a computer. Like, it's not that our system got better, we just opened a portal into Middle Earth and got Gandalf to take time out of his schedule to fix your fucking printer. Great. Now you can go print out that email from your Dad.

BRIANNA LEE:
I'm just going to say it: anyone who requires supernatural intervention to print should be using a Mac. Let Apple have those assholes.

STAN BANAS:
People who like Wizards should go hang out with Todd's mom.

ARLENE BRONSTEIN:
Todd was a wizard for Halloween once. I made him a pointy hat. Do you want to see a picture? Hold on…where did I put it?

Windows 95 introduced the now-infamous Blue Screen of Death (BSoD), which popped up whenever any type of fatal error occurred. But few know the story of the hard-working team that created it.

KARL SHINKMAN, *Fatal Exception Manager:*
You can't sugarcoat the fact that systems crash. Occasionally or frequently, they all go down at some point. So we decided that Win 95's crashes should be memorable. Iconic, even. The Fatal Exception Group made that possible.

TREVOR FERRIS, *Fatal Exception Engineer:*
We developed a screen that would scare the bejeezus out of you while giving you debugging data. It was known internally as "Basic Scary Operational Data."

SAMUEL OKADA, *QA Test Lead:*
QA called it "Bro, Systems Often Die." Customer Support called it "Because Stupid or Dumb."

KARL SHINKMAN:
Looked great, too. The designer nailed it.

FRANCIS BUSH, *Designer, Blue Screen of Death:*
I thought people would want to look at something primitive and also eye-searing whenever their computer was completely hosed. After focus group testing, I found the worst possible shade of blue.

KARL SHINKMAN:
Microsoft trademarked it. Have you ever seen a person wear that color? No. We own it.

FRANCIS BUSH:
That color haunts my dreams. That's how you know it's good.

See Figure.05 (page 76) for two first drafts of the Blue Screen of Death in untrademarked black and white.

Microsoft wanted users to feel just as special starting Windows 95 as they did crashing it. They approached ambient music pioneer Brian Eno with a strange request: to write a sound to play during startup.

BILL GATES:
At this point we were thinking about how to make the sound design
for Windows seem more with-it and artsy. So we got the guy who did
Music For Airports. He was avant-garde but not too niche. Everyone
can relate to music and airports.

BRIAN ENO, *Musician:*
I remember that ad agency sent me this crazy list of all the things they
wanted the sound to be. I was trying to think of stuff they'd left off but
it seemed like they'd covered every conceivable base. "Aspirational,"
"Classic," "Non-Neanderthal," "Futuristic," "Evocative of the Past."
And then they said it had to be a maximum of 3.25 seconds long.

KENNETH BRIGHT, *Advertising Executive:*
Let's just say there were a lot of people who needed to get something
on the list. It happens.

BRIAN ENO:
The last page completely baffled me. It was stuff like "crispy," "good
mouthfeel," and "low-sodium."

KENNETH BRIGHT:
Oh yeah, I remember that the lists got stuck together and we
accidentally sent the Win95 brief along with one for a new type of
McNugget that never went forward.

BRIAN ENO:
It's really hard to make something sound crispy on an analog
synthesizer. Not to mention moist. I kind of got into it, though. I ended
up making 84 different versions of the sound.

ANNE BORGESON, *Product Manager:*
Yeah, he sent all of them to us. Some of them had lyrics, which was
not in the brief. One was just him singing the word "crispy." There
were 20 of them that were clearly just 3.25 second bits of a longer
song about a cat in a forest. In the end, we chose the one called "The
Windows Sound."

BRIAN ENO:
Oh yeah, some of those were just "choices." I was lucky, they picked
the real one.

ANNE BORGESON:
I forgot what we did with the other 83.

JOSH COOPER:
Oh, I know what happened to the other ones. We found a Jaz drive full of them when we were doing the Windows Phone, so we threw a couple of them in as default ringtones. "Crispy" is my go-to meeting alert.

BRIAN ENO:
I'm proud of it. That one tiny piece of music had quite a life. The slowed-down trance remix of it ended up being a chillout room staple throughout the 90s.

MOBY, *Musician*:
I had a panic attack to that song in Ibiza one summer.

LISA K.:
I remember we played it backwards just to see what it would sound like. It sounded like another Brian Eno song. I was kind of bummed.

BRIAN ENO:
They did what? I'm not Judas Priest. Dorks.

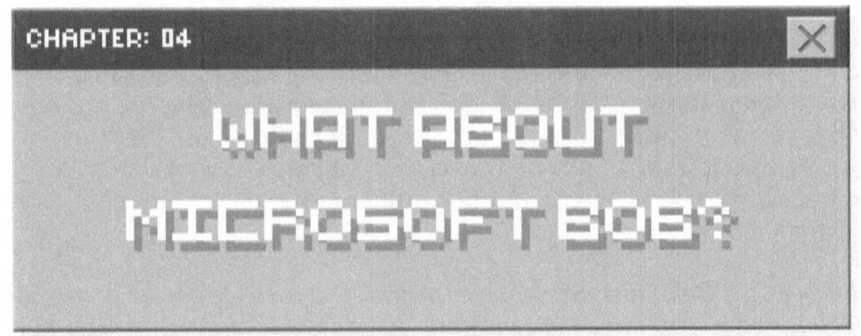

Hanging over the heads of the Win95 development team was the spectre of Microsoft Bob. Bob was an attempt to make an insanely simple user interface to run on top of Windows, aimed at people who were new to using computers. Basically, it sucked. We talked to the Bob team.

JANET VANDERWERFF, *VP Marketing*:
Bob was a groundbreaking way to access your computer. It changed the metaphor from a desktop to a friendlier, more accessible environment.

KEVIN HÖFFLER, *Bob Developer*:
The idea was that the desktop was your house and the applications were things in the house. So there'd be a room with all this crap in it and the crap would represent the applications.

JANET VANDERWERFF:
It made new users feel more comfortable, because they were interacting with ordinary objects, just like in the real world.

LYNNE CLEARY, *Bob Developer*:
Janet said that? With a straight face?

KEVIN HÖFFLER:
So if you wanted to open the calendar, you'd click on the calendar on the wall. Or you could look around and find the rolodex on the end table to open your contacts. And you could also spend a ton of time choosing which ugly room you wanted to be in. Woo.

JANET VANDERWERFF:
You could make the house look different from any one of our preloaded options. You could pick your own assistant to guide you through the programs. There was a sarcastic rat! And William Shakespeare!

LYNNE CLEARY:
Yeah, you had to pick a cartoon character to hang out with and they'd keep showing up with their stupid word bubbles asking you what you wanted to do. And you basically couldn't do anything until you told them, "okay." It was kind of like The Sims, only without any good choices and not fun. I blame the designers, particularly Joel Kim.

JOEL KIM, *Bob Designer*:
We named it Bob after my neighbor, a really, really old guy who kept saying he fought in the war and didn't trust computers.

KEVIN HÖFFLER:
Really old. You couldn't even ask him what war.

JOEL KIM:
The real Bob was hard of hearing and just not entirely there. I used to pick up his mail and try to get him to open the door and it would take forever.

KEVIN HÖFFLER:
In hindsight, we might have picked a less extreme user.

JOEL KIM:
One day I had a vision of a dog watching him at the computer, yelling, "Bob! Bob! What do you want to do? What are you trying to do? Are you trying to send an email? Are you writing your will? What? What are you doing? Do you want help with that? Bob? Are you okay? Tell me you're okay."

ARLENE BRONSTEIN:
They asked me to test it and I thought it was insulting.

JOSH COOPER, *Software Engineer*:
Oh God, Todd's mom was livid.

LYNNE CLEARY:
(sighs) Three years out of my life and it was gone by '96.

JOEL KIM:
Ironically, the real Bob died the day we shipped. So now we'll never know if he'd have been able to use it.

LANCE JACKSON, *Software Engineer*:
We were pretty close to delivery. And Bob was getting hammered in the press. What if 95 bombed like that? Todd wrote, in huge letters on the whiteboard, "Not Bob." We're not going to be Bob.

Windows 95 was not Bob. But some of the damage was already done. Microsoft Bob had a couple of long-lasting artifacts. One of the characters morphed into the Office Assistant, a cartoon of a paper clip who gave advice, known colloquially as Clippy. Clippy shot to fame several years later as part of Office 98, by ruining everyone's attempts to write a letter without interruption.

JANET VANDERWERFF:
I disagree with people who said nothing good came out of Bob. Whatever you think of Clippy, he had a cultural impact. It's publicity you can't pay for.

LYNNE CLEARY:
I don't know why everyone assumes a talking paper clip is a dude. Just saying.

KEVIN HÖFFLER:
I would scream, "Just Type the Letter Without Help. Jesus Christ, JUST TYPE THE GODDAMN LETTER WITHOUT HELP!"

See Figure.06 (page 77) for a typical Office Assistant.

JOEL KIM:
And then there's the other thing that came from Bob. We don't talk about the other thing.

JANET VANDERWERFF:
No comment.

LYNNE CLEARY:
Microsoft Bob was the project that gave the world Comic Sans. Seriously. Gino was in the font dungeon for months, working on some top-secret new font. But then Bob came out and it wasn't there. And a month later, we heard the screams.

GINO IPPOLITO, *Designer of Comic Sans*:
It was supposed to be an experiment. In its current form, it was never supposed to leave the font lab. I wasn't expecting it to mutate and go airborne. I would never do this on purpose. I'm a good person.

KEVIN HÖFFLER:
I heard he sold his soul to develop the next Arial. And this was the price.

JOEL KIM:
We thought it would stay contained within the lead-lined vault where they kept all the stuff from Bob. But it got breached during the party, it infected MovieMaker and the rest is history.

DONALD PRICE, *Director of the CFC (Centers for Font Control)*:
The world wasn't ready for it. We had no immunity. That font was on every break room fridge, every dorm bulletin board and every day care center's calendar. At this point, 96% of the world's surface has been infected by Comic Sans.

MELINDA GATES, *Former Marketing Manager for Microsoft Bob*:
Bill couldn't live with the guilt. And neither could I. Everyone eventually works on a project that fails, but there's no excuse for a disaster like Comic Sans. Bill and I talked and talked about how to make it right. We couldn't undo the damage, but we could use our wealth to make the world a better place. This eventually led us to start the Bill & Melinda Gates Foundation.

The Bill & Melinda Gates Foundation continues to donate billions of dollars to healthcare-related causes. Most recently, the foundation has focused on eradicating infectious diseases around the world.

BILL GATES, *Former Chairman and CEO of Microsoft*:
We do good work. But in all honesty, it's going to be far easier to eradicate malaria than Comic Sans. ▣

With the "Not Bob" mandate, Microsoft Chicago's team moved forward with development. And on the other side of the building, Microsoft Cairo's team continued to work in secrecy. Soon, the two projects would go head to head to determine the future of the Microsoft OS.

JOSH COOPER, *Software Engineer*:
At that point, we were running scared. The Cairo guys had the reputation for being the smartest people in the building. Did we even have a chance of beating them? What were they up to?

TODD BRONSTEIN, *VP, Microsoft Chicago*:
At the time, I couldn't even tell you what Cairo was. And that gave them a lot of leeway to do what they wanted. And Derek Unterberg was running things over there. Derek's managerial style is...unique.

DEREK UNTERBERG, *VP, Microsoft Cairo*:
I like to give my developers a lot of thinking time. Coding is an art form. My developers are making a masterpiece. And masterpieces take time. We need to allow time for elegance. And serendipity.

BRIANNA LEE, *Software Development Manager*:
He ran that department like a Montessori school. Their conference room had a sandbox in it. And everyone was afraid to go over there because of the hallway archery.

TODD BRONSTEIN:
Derek spent three years in Japan studying Zen archery. He used to practice with his eyes closed in the hallway.

LISA K., *Software Engineer*:
I heard they were all just sitting around doing pixy.

JOSH COOPER, *Software Engineer:*
That's the thing where you snort the contents of Pixy Stix. It's a stimulant. I'm not a fan. It burns and you sneeze in a variety of colors.

LANCE JACKSON, *Software Engineer:*
It's a performance enhancer, you can't deny it.

STAN BANAS, *Software Engineer:*
I used to do pixy. Scary stuff. I started using at Compaq, back in the day. That was like the Studio 54 of pixy use in the 80s. The tubes would pile up in the trash and they'd look the other way.

BRIANNA LEE:
I mean, I get it. At Harvard, I used to wake up and eat a pound of Sour Patch Kids every morning before class. But I have a kid now.

STAN BANAS:
We do have a Microsoft chapter of SA (Sucrose Anonymous). But most people think they can handle it. They're wrong.

BRIANNA LEE:
Every week, their status reports were just the words "object oriented file system." It was maddening.

JOSH COOPER:
Maybe those rollerblading assholes were onto something. Maybe Cairo would be a game-changer. Maybe they were going to blow us out of the water at the Bill meeting. Nobody knew.

TODD BRONSTEIN:
I couldn't stand all of Cairo's mystery shit, so I took a chance. I told Bill maybe it was time for both groups to present their interface demos. Maybe we should even do it at the same meeting. Winner takes all.

DEREK UNTERBERG:
We got a meeting invite from Bill. The time for greatness...was now.

Both groups prepared for trial by Gates.

LANCE JACKSON:
Bill Gates will destroy you if you don't have your shit together.

TODD BRONSTEIN:
Bill Gates can always find the weak point in your plan in a millisecond and then he'll spend the rest of the meeting just hammering on it.

BRIANNA LEE:
You don't leave a meeting with Bill. You get thrown out.

VLAD MICHAEL MURRAY, *Software Engineer*:
People would draw straws to see who had to sit directly across from Bill. He is the sun. You want to view him at an angle. I once brought a piece of cardboard with a pinhole in it to a Bill meeting, but I never had the balls to use it.

TODD BRONSTEIN:
I thought the presentation went relatively well. We had a couple of things that weren't a hundred percent there. Some overlapping on the Taskbar, some general sluggishness. The Blue Screen of Death was yellow. Wizard issues.

BRIANNA LEE:
I remember it got ugly when Todd said he wasn't sure about the Wizards, and Bill called him an idiot. Bill likes wizards.

BILL GATES, *Former Chairman and CEO of Microsoft*:
Of course I like the idea of wizards. Who doesn't want to live in a world where wizardry is possible? Next question.

STAN BANAS:
Bill yelled at us for like an hour, which was pretty good for Bill.

TODD BRONSTEIN:
Finally, I told Bill that it might not all be perfect, but my mom said it was just like the Apple Mac. And Bill Gates smiled. And it was good.

BRIANNA LEE:
Then Cairo went up. They started with a light show! They had matching silver polo shirts. I almost threw up from nerves.

LANCE JACKSON:
They talked for a long time about how revolutionary it was going to be. Then Bill cut them off and asked them to demo it. Oh dear God.

DEREK UNTERBERG:
I spent a great deal of time preparing my dance routine. I will never,
ever forgive Bill for cutting it short.

LANCE JACKSON:
It was obvious that nobody had tested Cairo. Like it'd been written
the night before or something.

BURT GWAR, *Cairo Developer*:
It was all written the night before. By me. Burt Gwar.

*Microsoft's post-mortem interviews revealed that Cairo's lack of supervision
and structure had been an ongoing issue throughout its development.*

BURT GWAR:
I got into programming after dropping out of grad school in physics.
I was never going to be a world class physicist, but I thought I had
the quantitative skills to create some amazing, life changing product.
Which led me to Microsoft, I guess? And I'd heard the Cairo group
were doing the craziest, most out-there projects. So I asked for a
transfer. Boy was I surprised.

ANDREW KEELER, *Program Manager, Cairo*:
Oh right, Burt! Ha! We got him so good.

BURT GWAR:
Shortly after I arrived, I was told that Cairo was a front for a
skunkworks project to build a time machine. They gave me an office
and told me to design the interface. I did that for eight months and
then I found out they were just fucking with me.

ANDREW KEELER:
I can't believe how long he kept working on that.

BURT GWAR:
At least I was being productive. There were two guys who just sat
in their offices writing bullshit code comments. You're supposed to
write comments to explain the code to other developers, they're not
there to act as a blank canvas for all your repressed creative desires.

MARVIN BREE, *Cairo Developer*:
I hate Xander. He can't even format a comment correctly. It's
supposed to be /* and then you draw a picture of Cindy Margolis,
then you say whatever you have to say.

XANDER HOWELLS, *Cairo Developer*:
Idiot. Your don't use comments for ASCII art, you use them to
explore the human condition through poetry.

MARVIN BREE:
I think it's totally valid to consider your code an art object in and of
itself. If you want to draw Cindy Margolis as the Mona Lisa in the
comments, you should.

BURT GWAR:
Oh right, "code as art." Their code was suitable for framing. And
that's it.

See Figure.07 (page 78) for a sample of Cairo's code comments.

ANDREW KEELER:
Hey, Xander once won a Pushcart Prize for his comments on
Windows NT 3.0. It was a sestina about how much Marvin sucked
for drinking the last Tab.

ADAM LODGE, *Cairo Tester*:
I was assigned to test Cairo's code. I had pretty much nothing to do.
There were usually more comments than code. Though it was nice to
watch Xander evolve as a poet.

DEREK UNTERBERG:
I think they fulfilled an important function in our group: keeping
me entertained.

BURT GWAR:
So I'd just wasted eight months and it didn't look like anyone else
had done anything either. I got a meeting with Derek and asked him
if Cairo was a real product that was going to ship. He said of course
Cairo was real. He said he'd jump off a bridge if we didn't ship.

In fact, months into the project, Cairo had yet to define its key features.

ANDREW KEELER:
We had a lot of possible directions to narrow down. I was messing
around with a thing where Cairo could generate infinite windows
within other windows. If you looked at it too long, it would give
you vertigo.

BURT GWAR:
After a while I gave up. I just sat staring at the wall, wondering if time travel was really possible.

ANDREW KEELER:
Then Todd Bronstein got past The Archer, which was what we called Derek in "Zen mode."

TODD BRONSTEIN:
I went over there to borrow a CD burner and everyone was doing yoga to the soundtrack from *Koyaanisqatsi*. That's when I started to think that Cairo was vaporware.

ANDREW KEELER:
The next day we got the meeting invite from Bill. We were hosed.

BURT GWAR:
The night before the meeting I stayed up and drank a lot of Mountain Dew, did a bunch of pixy and wrote the preliminary kernel and file system. For the interface, I threw in parts of the interface from the time machine and the window within window thing. It was insane, but it was better than nothing.

ANDREW KEELER:
Burt pulled a whole system out of his ass in one night. I was impressed. And I thought the time machine thing looked pretty boss.

In the meeting with Bill Gates, the Chicago team were flummoxed by how ill-prepared Cairo was for the presentation.

TODD BRONSTEIN:
One guy presented a couple of hacked together bits and pieces of stuff that were kind of on point but looked weirdly like a time machine. The architecture was okay, but Bill was flabbergasted at the interface. He said, "This is supposed to be the future of Windows. Why does it look like a time machine running Windows 3.1?"

BRIANNA LEE:
And then some other guy showed him some weird window within window thing and Bill said, "What the fuck, is this a screensaver?"

STAN BANAS:
It was even worse when he tried to open a window and instead of a filename, it was a poem.

BRIANNA LEE:
Bill said, "What have you guys been doing for eight months?" Derek said, "We're working up to an object oriented file system" and then Bill threw them out.

DEREK UNTERBERG:
That was a tough one. I had to tell my team that I wasn't angry, but I was very, very disappointed in them. I told them in a haiku written in the kernel.

ANDREW KEELER:
So Bill killed Cairo. Or, he gave it to the Outlook people, which is more like he killed it and then set it on fire and then shot it with a bazooka. A couple of blackened shards of it eventually landed in NT 4.0. And we were transferred to Chicago. Fuuuuuuuck.

LANCE JACKSON:
Oh, the sweetness of watching those dudes get their Todd-boxes and having to drink our soda. Bill also took their skates.

BRIANNA LEE:
We rode home in the van, and they were just walking.

TODD BRONSTEIN:
So it was decided. The future was going to look like Windows 95. And that was when it really got nuts. ⊠

The real triumph of Windows 95 was its marketing and public relations campaign. Part of the campaign was traditional advertising; part of it was creating an avalanche of marketing and PR stunts.

WENDY PRATT, *Creative Director:*
We needed the Windows 95 campaign to be legendary. We had to outdo our blowout for Windows 3.1. A bunch of us spent weeks in the conference room brainstorming. When you do that, you just have to go for it. There are no bad ideas.

VLAD MICHAEL MURRAY, *Software Engineer:*
There are plenty of bad ideas. And they had all of them.

GRANT SHAPIRO, *Copywriter:*
We thought about a negative campaign against Apple. They had the Trash. We had the Recycling Bin. So we'd run ads about how Microsoft is environmentally friendly while Apple is polluting your hard drive. Then Engineering got on our case.

VLAD MICHAEL MURRAY:
Todd sent me upstairs to explain that putting files in the Trash does not hurt the environment. There is no such thing as a "data landfill."

WENDY PRATT:
I suggested we get the Guinness Book of World Records to come out and give Microsoft the record for World's Longest Filename.

GRANT SHAPIRO:
Right, and then Engineering told us that it was only 255 characters max, and we couldn't just make a special one for publicity.

VLAD MICHAEL MURRAY:
I told them: it's not like pi, it doesn't go on indefinitely.

GRANT SHAPIRO:
Lame.

VLAD MICHAEL MURRAY:
At some point, Marketing just started making features up.

WENDY PRATT:
We storyboarded a commercial that claimed Windows 95 came
with a subscription to virtual reality. We were going to hire the
Lawnmower Man! And then Engineering had to tank that one, too.

VLAD MICHAEL MURRAY:
A subscription to virtual reality? What does that even mean? I think
that's when I started using pixy.

GEOFFREY MEADOWS, *Account Executive*:
Finally, I said, "Let's just try every idea we've thrown out because it
would be too crazy and expensive." And we did.

PINKIE MILLER, *PR Director*:
Some were pretty traditional, like skywriting "Where do you want to
go today?" in key markets.

PHIL SCHAEFER, *PR Coordinator*:
Blimps. We had an assortment of blimps.

MITCH VOORHEES, *PR Manager*:
We were going to release flocks of birds that would fly over cities in
the shape of the Microsoft logo. But there were execution issues.

HENRY STAFFORD, *Animal Trainer*:
It is very hard to train birds to fly in a specific formation. It is also
hard to find birds that match Microsoft's logo colors. Most of the
birds that are the right color don't fly in formation and they sure as
hell won't fly in a group full of unfamiliar birds of several different
species. It was madness.

DARLENE GILL, *Assistant Trainer*:
Just bloody feathers everywhere.

HENRY STAFFORD:
We ended up paying a ridiculous amount of money for a flock of
genetically engineered albino ducks and dyed them to match. But
then the ducks wouldn't fly in the right order and it all looked like
crap. Finally, the ASPCA stepped in and shut us down.

PINKIE MILLER:
We paid the fine. Cost of doing business. I don't know, I think there's
still something in that idea.

JAMIE VORPAHL, *ASPCA Representative*:
There are a lot of confused ducks in Redmond. Even now.

*Microsoft made its very first television ads for Windows 95. They hired the
advertising firm Wieden + Kennedy to develop a campaign, and even more
importantly, a theme song.*

JAKE ROBERTS, *Campaign Manager*:
We knew we were going to do a bunch of shots of people using
Windows all over the place. You know, business, business, business,
screenshots, cityscape, café, more screenshots, blue collar workers
doing stuff, screenshots, multiethnic people doing business on trains,
that kind of thing. But what was the song?

TED YORK, *Lead Copywriter*:
We sat there and sat there. I threw a stress ball at Jeff. He threw it
back at me. I threw it and it bounced off Aaron's head. He threw it at
Jeff. Jeff threw it at me. I was like, let's not start this up again.

JEFF CAMPBELL, *Copywriter*:
I was thinking like, *whatever, I don't want to work for this place anymore,
I want to work for some cool startup.*

AARON FORD, *Copywriter*:
We kept throwing out ideas. It was coming in fits and starts. And ups
and downs. And starts and ups.

TED YORK:
Then Matty called to say he couldn't come in because his car
wouldn't start –

JEFF CAMPBELL:
Up to now, he'd been driving this crap car because he was saving up
for a starter home.

AARON FORD:
And then some guy with a jackhammer outside yelled, "Start it up!"

TED YORK:
And then...it hit us.

AARON FORD:
Mötley Crüe's "Kickstart My Heart." Eureka!

TED YORK:
But we couldn't get the rights.

JEFF CAMPBELL:
And then I was like, isn't there a Rolling Stones song called "Start Me Up?"

TED YORK:
We had to look it up, but yes.

The Rolling Stones had never licensed a song for advertising. The negotiation process was intense. Published accounts claim the negotiations were performed by intermediaries. However, according to our interviews, they were performed by Mick Jagger, Keith Richards, and Bill Gates himself.

MICK JAGGER, *The Rolling Stones*:
I've always been against licensing. It's a sellout move.

KEITH RICHARDS, *The Rolling Stones*:
Mick hated the idea. But I had lost a lot of money in the collectibles market. Beanie Babies. They're my heroin. I needed what you Americans call a buttload of money. It's a good thing I picked up the phone when Microsoft called.

ELI HALLMAN, *Lead Counsel, Microsoft*:
It was really weird that he picked up. I was expecting a business manager.

KEITH RICHARDS:
Yeah, Rupert was getting lunch and I was just sitting around his office, checking my email.

BILL GATES, *Former Chairman and CEO of Microsoft*:
I thought it was crazy. Where were we going to get that kind of
money? Just for some song? We were doing our own thing. Why not
have someone in-house make up a cool MIDI and play that? Or get
some newer band, like Ace of Base? Microsoft: I Saw the Start Button.
Microsoft: All That She Wants Is Another OS.

ELI HALLMAN:
I told Bill the Rolling Stones were big fans of Microsoft and wanted
to be associated with cutting edge technology.

KEITH RICHARDS:
Yeah, we made up some bullshit about how we were big technology
fans and that made it more or less okay for Mick. But Mick wanted to
make sure they were serious.

MICK JAGGER:
We had them fly to us. We had them sit in a room with not enough
chairs. Just messing with them. We required everyone to wear canary
yellow, which made them look like wankers. We asked them to bring
a suitcase full of money.

BILL GATES:
I said, "You do know how much Microsoft is worth, correct? Why do
you need to see cash?"

MICK JAGGER:
We said, "Suitcase full of money or no deal."

KEITH RICHARDS:
So anyway, they show up on the first day with a suitcase full of cash,
probably $200,000. We reached under the table and brought out our
suitcase full of cash, which contained $500,000 and said, "Ours is
bigger, come back tomorrow."

ELI HALLMAN:
I could hear Bill Gates screaming at them all the way down the hall.
But we kept talking and wired for more cash.

KEITH RICHARDS:
They came back the next day with a bigger suitcase but we'd
already swapped ours out for an even bigger one. Ha ha! We sent
them home again.

BILL GATES:
Unbelievable.

KEITH RICHARDS:
And we're not idiots. We checked every time to make sure the whole
briefcase was full of cash and they weren't just buying a bigger
suitcase. One day there was a bunch of newspaper on the bottom
and we sent them back.

MICK JAGGER:
Finally, they brought one that was a lot bigger than what we had.
And we made the deal.

BILL GATES:
I can't give an exact number, but it was 3 million dollars.

MICK JAGGER:
And then there was round two. We weren't going to tell people we'd
sold out for a measly 3 million dollars. We planned to leak to the
press that the song had gone for 50 million dollars. That's how you
set a market price. Our business manager is a genius.

BILL GATES:
That's when I walked out. I was not going to look like a chump.
But they called back and I talked to our lawyers and eventually we
made the leak into a deal point. I talked them down to lying about
the price in the range of 12-14 million dollars. The press ate it up.
The price was just the right amount of crazy to make us look like
we were operating on a different scale entirely, but not like we were
throwing money away. Their business manager is a genius.

ELI HALLMAN:
Did I mention that their business manager was named Prince
Rupert Louis Ferdinand Frederick Constantine Lofredo Leopold
Herbert Maximilian Hubert John Henry zu Löwenstein-Wertheim-
Freudenberg? He was the first man in Britain to undergo name
enlargement surgery.

BILL GATES:
After we closed, we invited Prince Rupert to visit the Microsoft campus.

JOSH COOPER, *Software Engineer:*
I got to give him the tour. He really is an aristocrat. He asked me
which way to the vomitorium. When I told him we didn't have a
room for just vomiting alcohol, he told me he'd build us one. It's rad.
Good god, that man has stories.

KANWAR KHAN, *Software Engineer:*
He truly is an expert on partying. This was the man who had been
observing Mick Jagger partying since 1968. That's as close as we
would ever get to being rock stars. Watching him scoff at our pixy.

*Running the public relations end of the launch was the legendary and
charismatic Sharon Davis. Her task was to make every magazine and
newspaper editor, every Wall Street analyst, every TV host in the country
and abroad want to talk about Windows 95. To do so, she called upon a
network she'd been building for years.*

VINCENT CHU, *Staff Writer, Wired:*
Sharon Davis knows everyone. She sees everything. It's scary. How
does she do that?

SHARON DAVIS, *Public Relations Legend:*
It's all about relationships. And maintaining relationships. And that
requires access, to people and to information. Anyone can keep a
contact database and send a birthday card. We wanted more. So we
got help.

JOHN GARY, *Microsoft PR Recruiter:*
My job was to locate people who were willing to be assets for the
cause. Moles, basically. Ordinary, smart people who would just go
about their lives while working their way into key areas.

CARLA WHEELER, *Public Relations Mole:*
I was at Wharton. I came home from class one day and there was a
rose on my desk and an engraved invitation to a party at an obscure
Philadelphia club. I don't know how they got into my apartment, but
I decided to check it out. That was my initiation.

BJORN AVERY, *Public Relations Mole:*
I was a journalism major at Northwestern and my professor called
me in for one of the "special" meetings the grad students whispered
about. I thought I was being recruited for the CIA. But it was way
bigger than that.

JOHN GARY:
We got them young, business school, journalism school. We scooped up English majors during their crappy publishing internships. We had eyes on the street: bouncers, club kids, florists, deli workers, those people who spin signs on street corners...

ACE PUNCHER, *Private Eye***:**
I was a down on my luck private dick. Skip tracing, divorces. Nothing interesting. And then a woman walked in. She had a face that could...she had legs like...yeah, she was pretty average looking. She said, "Whatever they're paying you, I'll double it." I said, "Who are you talking about?"

SHARON DAVIS:
The idea was to know our targets better than they knew themselves.

ACE PUNCHER:
They had me sift through public records, which was more of a deal because this was pre-internet. Who's married, who's divorced, who gave birth, who bought a house. And to get pictures of all of those things.

SHARON DAVIS:
We'd get daily reports from dead drops around the city and compile them into dossiers.

BJORN AVERY:
They wanted to know my editor's fondest wishes, his secret dreams. Who he was dating and why. Who he wanted to be dating. What he really, really wanted for Christmas.

SHARON DAVIS:
But we wouldn't get them the gift. That's unethical. We'd have an agent lure a friend or family member into a van, hypnotize them, and plant the suggestion that they buy the gift for our target. And then our mole would hypnotize the target into subconsciously associating the gift with Microsoft.

CARLA WHEELER:
I was weirded out by that at first, but when I thought about it, I realized that we were really just improving lives.

JOHN GARY:
Some of it was just Sharon's gift for friendship. She knew how to be there for people. With our help.

SHARON DAVIS:
I set up a lot of blind dates. Officiated at a lot of weddings. Took a lot of people to the airport. I am ordained in several religions and the Universal Life Church.

JOHN GARY:
By 1994, Sharon had moved up 20 slots on the list of popular baby names. That was all us.

SHARON DAVIS:
When you think of love, sex, family, dreams, anything positive in your life, we'd want you to think Microsoft made that possible. And then write a piece on Windows.

JOHN GARY:
And they did.

Microsoft broke new ground by producing a VHS instructional video, which explained Windows 95 to the casual user via the new medium of "Cyber Sitcom." In a casting coup, Jennifer Aniston and Matthew Perry from the cast of a normal sitcom called Friends signed on to star, as themselves.

WAYNE RILEY, *New Brunswick Video*:
This was our first time working with that kind of budget – our only previous tech video involved a claymation dog who barked out DOS commands. We had several directors come in and pitch.

JULIAN BOUCHARD, *Director*:
We sent it to John Singleton with a basket of cookies. No response. We sent it to Oliver Stone, who was out of our price range thanks to *Nixon*. We had lunch with Hal Hartley, but he kept talking about Martin Donovan, then realized he was at the wrong meeting. Spielberg would only do it if John Williams could score the startup sounds, but Eno was already locked in. David Lynch wanted total creative control, so that wasn't happening. So I just directed it myself.

WAYNE RILEY:
My brother-in-law is a writer, so we brought him on to write the script.

DESMOND YAZ, *Screenwriter*:
Up to that point, I had been writing technical manuals for Lotus 1-2-3, but Wayne said, "It's the same thing, you're perfect!" and I got the job. That script was tough. To clear my head, I skipped town and crashed in the guest house at Art Garfunkel's place on Martha's Vineyard.

ART GARFUNKEL, *Musician*:
Someone broke into our place that summer.

WAYNE RILEY:
Desmond did a pretty good job, but eventually we had to call John Sayles in to fix a couple of things. He insisted on working uncredited. I heard he used the money to fund *Lone Star*.

JULIAN BOUCHARD:
The original concept was that it was a video within a video. Matthew Perry and Jennifer Aniston show up to Bill Gates's office to talk about being in the instructional video for Windows 95. They are gradually seduced by its incredible features.

WAYNE RILEY:
Microsoft originally suggested we use Paul Reiser and Helen Hunt from *Mad About You*, but Helen Hunt had an existing relationship with Linux.

DESMOND YAZ:
I wrote it for Matthew Perry and Jennifer Aniston. There was never anyone else in my mind who could pull off these parts. No one.

DAVID SCHWIMMER, *Actor:*
I can't tell you how insulting that is.

WAYNE RILEY:
This was season 2 of *Friends*. They were totally affordable.

JULIAN BOUCHARD:
In the end, they would only agree to do it if they could look unimpressed in almost every shot. But it still had to be funny. It was a sitcom.

WAYNE RILEY:
At one point Jennifer Aniston calls a floppy disk a "flappy disc." My joke!

DESMOND YAZ:
Not true.

JULIAN BOUCHARD:
I don't remember who came up with that, but it was genius.

JENNIFER ANISTON, *Cyber Sitcom Co-Star:*
I don't think I got enough credit for selling that line. It's so hard to sell garbage. That's acting.

WAYNE RILEY:
Bill Gates never appears in the video. And believe me, we begged, but it didn't work out.

BILL GATES, *Former Chairman and CEO of Microsoft*:
My agent advised me to pass. He was trying to get me into features. Also, at the time, I was running Microsoft.

WAYNE RILEY:
Plus, they wouldn't allow us to film in Bill Gates's office, so we had to imaginatively recreate it.

JULIAN BOUCHARD:
I said, "Glass blocks! Give me more glass blocks! Make it look like a futuristic dentist's office."

GILLIAN MADDEN, *Prop Master*:
I argued for the ergonomic keyboard. I mean, it's frigging Bill Gates!

Various characters introduce Matthew Perry and Jennifer Aniston to Windows 95, including Bill Gates's secretary, Bernice Keppleman, Boris the Window Washer, a yuppie called The Chipster, tween videogame whiz Joystick Johnny, Matthew Perry's stoner friend Tim, Tim's grunge band, and a controversial character, Chinese restaurant delivery guy, Jeff Lee.

DESMOND YAZ:
Yeah, I wanted to show a broad cross-section of people representing the diverse intended audience for Windows 95. But after the first draft, someone pointed out that all the characters were white. I thought, *Asians use computers. Maybe Jen and Matt can order from a Chinese restaurant – by e-fax! And then meet a friendly delivery guy who knows computers.* Kill two birds with one stone.

WAYNE RILEY:
I thought we were being evenhandedly satirical. We had one of every stereotype: Jewish, Russian, Yuppie, Skater, Asian Delivery Guy, Grunge Band. Or at least we had every stereotype that you could get away with in 1995.

JORDAN CHEUNG, *Actor:*
My agent sent me the sides for Jeff Lee and I immediately passed.
I mean, he comes in to deliver Chinese takeout on his bicycle that's
decorated to look like a dragon. He's dressed like David Carradine in
Kung Fu. And he makes karate moves and calls people "grasshopper."
It had everything but a gong.

WALTER YEE, *Actor:*
I went in for it and they wanted it "more Asian." Jesus Christ. I gave
everyone the finger and left. No regrets.

WAYNE RILEY:
Oh yeah, Jeff Lee... Every guy we auditioned turned it down saying
that it was an offensive stereotype. So we got a blond guy to do it and
kept everything else the same.

JULIAN BOUCHARD:
It's not racist if it's obviously a white guy. It's also not racist if it's
not convincing.

GILLIAN MADDEN:
It was a little weird. He came off as one of those weird Asiaphile guys
who runs a strip mall kung fu studio. But whatever, he was hot.

KEVIN DEWEY, *Actor:*
Wait, Jeff Lee was supposed to be Asian?

DESMOND YAZ:
The video was quite progressive. Jennifer Aniston beats the sexist little
troll at 3D Pinball, even though she's a girl.

JULIAN BOUCHARD:
We had a pinball double for Jennifer. She actually had a pinball
rider; she isn't allowed to be shown playing pinball. Because she has
thumb warts.

WAYNE RILEY:
Yeah, that's why you so rarely see her play games or type in movies.
They were able to shoot around them on *Friends,* but that's multicam,
not a lot of hand shots. We thought we could get around it by having
her wear green screen colored thumb covers. But in the end, we didn't
have the budget to CGI in another pair of thumbs.

JULIAN BOUCHARD:
Her double was actually my wife, Sasha, who is legitimately a pinball wizard. As a young woman, she'd been coached by the technical advisor for *Tommy*. Sasha learned to beat 3D Pinball in one night.

SASHA SMITH-BOUCHARD, *Legitimate Pinball Wizard*:
It's not that hard a game. Plus, no tilting.

JULIAN BOUCHARD:
The pinball issue wasn't nearly as difficult to deal with as Matthew Perry's catchphrase rider. The original script used the phrase "Could you *be* any more…" six times, but we were negotiated down to one use. Some of the ones we cut:

Could you *be* any more started up?
Could I *be* any more able to fax electronically?
Could you *be* any more terrible at 3D pinball?
Could Windows 95 *be* any more user-friendly?
Could you *be* any more trapped in this computer?

WAYNE RILEY:
Yeah, the creators of *Friends* were worried about that phrase peaking before season 3 even happened.

DESMOND YAZ:
We tried to reference as many popular things as possible. The Information Superhighway, grunge, rave parties.

BRETT PETERS, *Video Clerk*
I appreciated the use of pop cultural references. Microsoft really had their cursor on the pulse of American society.

CORY LASTIMOSA, *TV Blogger*:
For me, it ruined *Friends*. Well, Ross and Rachel ruined *Friends*, but this did not help.

DAVID SCHWIMMER:
Again, very insulting.

The musical cues were particularly unusual and involved a secret celebrity guest.

JULIAN BOUCHARD:
At the table read we were having trouble with the jokes landing. We
were worried that the audience wouldn't be on board with the Cyber
Sitcom concept, especially with no laugh track. So my idea was to
underline every punch line with some sort of musical sting. And
Seinfeld was my favorite show, so I hired a bassist.

WAYNE RILEY:
The bassist was actually Flea from the Red Hot Chili Peppers. He was
a fan and wanted to get involved.

FLEA, *Bassist, The Red Hot Chili Peppers*:
That was one weird-ass gig. But I did it for free. Bill Gates got me out
of a jam once, so I owed him one.

SAM HUNTINGTON, *Actor, "Joystick Johnny"*:
When we were shooting, Flea was actually standing just off camera
and playing live. It was rad.

WAYNE RILEY:
Yeah, and he's basically playing the riff from *Seinfeld*. That, we got
in trouble for. There was a court case on whether playing a bunch of
random bass stings was copyrightable. Our argument was that we
were using it differently by playing it after every joke.

JULIAN BOUCHARD:
I was impressed at how good Jennifer and Matt were at holding after
each joke. Those multicam guys are pros.

HARRY VONS, *Composer*:
I thought it was jarring that the score would switch between the
comedy stings and the "reverential Microsoft music" every time they
showed the computer screen. But whatever, I got paid.

Steve Kokkinos, from Microsoft Quality Assurance, was on hand as a
technical consultant. His presence was not appreciated.

STEVE KOKKINOS, *Microsoft QA Lead*:
I was on set with a mandate from Bill Gates himself to preserve the
technical accuracy of the video.

JULIAN BOUCHARD:
Oh god, Microsoft guy.

STEVE KOKKINOS:
When I showed up they said, "Oh good, Microsoft guy!"

BRICE DIPASQUALE, *Unemployed Nerd*:
If you pay attention, you notice that they don't save the filled in
Chinese Menu before they fax it.

STEVE KOKKINOS:
It was correct in the script they gave me, but then they didn't shoot it!

JULIAN BOUCHARD:
It was the last shot of the last day and we were running over. I didn't
have time for Microsoft guy and his shit-fits. So we moved on.
Whatever, people get it.

STEVE KOKKINOS:
He said nobody would notice. I lost it. I told them I'd tell Bill. They
kicked me off the set. Whenever I'm shown that scene, I need a Xanax.

JULIAN BOUCHARD:
He was right, in the end. We got letters about that. And many e-faxes.

DESMOND YAZ:
At the end of the Cyber Sitcom, Jennifer Aniston and Matthew Perry
press a red button that sucks all of the characters, who represent
features of the software, back into the computer. It is the ultimate
shutdown. Actually that's not a safe way to shut down your computer,
but, you know, artistic license. I had to fight for that ending.

STEVE KOKKINOS:
Aaaaaaaugh!

MATTHEW PERRY, *Cyber Sitcom Co-Star*:
I didn't get that. That's deep.

BRICE DIPASQUALE:
Yeah, I call bullshit.

WAYNE RILEY:
We turned in the rough cut and then we found out Microsoft guy *did*
rat us out to Bill. So we had to shoot a whole second half, which was
just a bunch of lists of Microsoft Features. I don't know a single person
who's watched it.

FRANZ BREUER, *Microsoft Enthusiast*:
According to legend, at the end of the video is the location and the
unlock code for a vault with a million dollars inside. Microsoft wanted
to see if anyone would watch it the whole way through. The prize
has gone unclaimed, because no one can sit through the whole video
without falling asleep. I've tried at least 20 times.

WAYNE RILEY:
That video launched some impressive careers. Joystick Johnny went
on to fame and fortune on *Veronica Mars*.

SAM HUNTINGTON:
Yeah, that video was a turning point for me. Who knew?

DESMOND YAZ:
I think the video was ahead of its time. Just look at the part about
cat photos.

PETER BENSON, *Actor, "The Chipster"*:
My character of "The Chipster," whom I modeled on Scooter from *The
Muppet Show* and Peter Scolari from *Newhart*, shows Jennifer Aniston
how to access cat photos on MSN.

JULIAN BOUCHARD:
It's amazing. Our video predicted the rise and dominance of cat
photos as a primary source of entertainment on the internet.

JENNIFER ANISTON:
Hmmmm.

Microsoft made 5 million copies of the video and sold them at retail outlets.

BRETT PETERS:
I remember my entire family gathering in the living room to watch
the video every Thursday night. It was our version of Must See TV.
Of course, we turned it off after the sitcom part. Who wants to watch
"Top Features of Windows 95"?

BRICE DIPASQUALE:
I watched to the end. Office for Windows comes to life as a giant
Godzilla monster and destroys Chicago. No, wait, that was a dream I
had. Have I fallen asleep every time I've tried to watch that video?

JULIAN BOUCHARD:
The Microsoft Windows 95 Video Guide. My masterpiece. ▨

Any software project is in a constant state of debugging. Windows 95 was no exception, with over 6000 bugs logged by developers, testers, and users.

LANCE JACKSON, *Software Engineer:*
As a developer, most of your time is spent debugging. And we created some spectacular bugs.

BRIANNA LEE, *Software Development Manager:*
Early on, you'd hit the "Start" button, and everything would stop working. The irony was lost on no one.

KANWAR KHAN, *Software Engineer:*
For a while, when you ran more than three applications, it would send a fax. What?

STAN BANAS, *Software Engineer:*
And Plug and Play was buggy as hell. It got such a bad rap after release, people called it "Plug and Pray." But they had no idea. When we were testing it, we called it "Plug and Hit the Deck."

VLAD MICHAEL MURRAY, *Software Engineer:*
For a while, when you tried to install an HP printer, someone in your office would die. But we knocked that one down in a couple days and only lost a few interns.

JOSH COOPER, *Software Engineer:*
I remember one day there was a general protection fault and it blew out a window on the third floor.

LISA K., *Software Engineer:*
That was a goose.

LANCE JACKSON:
There was a bug where the Blue Screen of Death displayed
in German for no reason. Unless you were running German
Windows and then it displayed in Portuguese. By the way, a
fascinating language...

BRIANNA LEE:
We'd stay up for days, just playing whack-a-mole with whatever
craziness had come up. It was worse when it was your mistake.
You'd look at it and look at it and get as far as you could and then
eventually, you'd call in Sherman from Testing. He always found it.

STAN BANAS:
I hate Sherman. Smug bastard.

SHERMAN SANDERS, *Software Tester*:
Attention to detail. Look it up.

JOSH COOPER:
Sherman was a developer for a while. It's weird: He could find a
bug in 10 seconds, but everything he wrote was insanely buggy.
Complicated guy.

BRIANNA LEE:
I mean, eventually we shifted him to Testing. Then he became even
more insufferable.

SHERMAN SANDERS:
I am legend.

LISA K.:
The worst bug reports come from Marketing. It's stuff like, "I was in
the middle of opening Word and I was drinking a peppermint latte
and then the blue thing happened. I was also running Minesweeper.
Does that do anything? You know what? Just come over here and I'll
show you." Ugh.

VLAD MICHAEL MURRAY:
And you go all the way upstairs to look at it and they can't make it
happen again.

GRANT SHAPIRO, *Copywriter*:
I'd say dude, it was just doing it!

JANET VANDERWERFF, *VP Marketing*:
I think when Engineering comes up, they do something that makes
it hide. Like, my machine can sense their anger and just won't give
them anything. Not even the time of day.

BRIANNA LEE:
Their clocks were always wrong for some reason. How hard it is to
set a clock?

ORVILLE CRABTREE, *Janitor, Windows Group*:
I squashed plenty of bugs. If you're going to leave the office with
soda cans half empty on your desk or pizza boxes on top of the
copier, you're going to get roaches and you're going to get ants.

JOSH COOPER:
It's not like it stopped anyone.

*Various builds, from alpha to beta to release candidates, were tested and
the bugs were logged to be corrected by developers, roughly in order of
importance. Except for certain special cases.*

BRIANNA LEE:
Most of the time when we talk about bugs, we're talking about
malfunctioning code. But then there's the other thing.

KANWAR KHAN:
We call them "superbugs."

SHERMAN SANDERS:
Sometimes a bug is so huge and so egregious that it becomes sentient
and takes on physical form. It possesses a human being, usually a
junior level tester.

ADAM LODGE, *Cairo Tester*:
Someone young and relatively unformed becomes transfixed by its
sheer awfulness.

VLAD MICHAEL MURRAY:
In this particular instance, when you tried to change the desktop
background, it always stretched it to the wrong aspect ratio. Then,
your eyes would start bleeding. Every light bulb within a hundred
yards would explode, and strange dogs would inexplicably start
sprinting towards your location. Sherman ran over to our group,
yelling that we had a live one.

SHERMAN SANDERS:
The bug had taken over the body of a kid named Miles, who was
only there on loan from Word for Windows. Poor bastard. He was
running around the area unplugging everything, kicking over chairs,
destroying people's Ship-it awards.

BURT GWAR, *Cairo Developer*:
It was bad. He kicked a soda onto Todd's machine. He stopped a
version mid-compile. Well, it was shitty code and it wasn't compiling
anyway, but the soda didn't help.

LISA K.:
He also grew six arms, tiny wings, and a hundred eyes. Did anyone
else mention that?

ADAM LODGE:
At that point we need to hunt down the bug and exorcise it. And
that's when we call in the Bug Squad.

SHERMAN SANDERS:
The Bug Squad is an elite group of testers who are familiar with
psychology, shamanism, and Visual Basic. Their job is to restrain the
bug and get it to the basement arena under Building 8, so that Bill
can...handle it.

JACE WILCOX, *Retired Developer*:
Yeah. I spent some time on the squad. Trained others. But you can't
do it forever. It's a high burnout position. You have to be willing to
do what's necessary to get the bug subdued.

STAN BANAS:
So they managed to chase the bug to the server room and brain him
with the user manual for Microsoft Access. They wrapped him up in
an Encarta Blanket and carried him to Building 8.

BRIANNA LEE:
It's kind of crazy how much people looked forward to this. There is
an ululating cry that goes up and down the halls. Thinking about it
still gives me chills.

JOSH COOPER:
Bill enters the arena. There is silence.

LANCE JACKSON:
Here's the process: the bug is brought before Bill and he evaluates
it. The crowd waits, and then Bill gives it a thumbs up or a thumbs
down. The thumbs down means he's going to destroy it. Thumbs up,
it becomes a feature.

KANWAR KHAN:
And that's where pivot tables came from.

BRIANNA LEE:
People would wager how long it would take Bill to finish it off. We
honestly were starting to wonder if he should retire from the arena;
if we lost Bill, we lost everything. But Steve Ballmer wasn't ready. He
didn't have the moves.

STEVE BALLMER, *Former President and CEO of Microsoft, But No
Bill Gates*:
I have great moves. I had great moves at the time. But it's political.
You have to have the confidence of the masses.

STAN BANAS:
Bill lets the bug scuttle around the arena. He taunts it. He asks it
questions. He makes it explain itself. He slowly picks away at its
defenses. He lets it wear itself out and then he charges.

VLAD MICHAEL MURRAY:
Oh man, Bill has a great finishing move. He looks the bug straight in
the eye and says I'M MICROSOFT. BUT YOU'RE MICROSOFTER.
And then he headbutts it, picks it up and hurls it through a wall
of OS/2 machines. At that point, the tester usually wakes up and
is carried to the Microsoft infirmary for observation. The bug-like
features disappear in about a week.

BURT GWAR:
I think it's cathartic, watching the bug go down. It releases group
tensions and exonerates our failures as developers.

SHERMAN SANDERS:
After the bug is defeated, we write up the ticket and we hang it in
the cafeteria. There is a dance, but outsiders are not allowed to see it.

KANWAR KHAN:
And then the Microsoft Chorus adds a verse to their epic ballad "Bill
Gates, Destroyer of Bugs."

ADAM LODGE:
Every now and then a bug would be defeated almost instantly. Then Bill would yell at us for bringing him bullshit errors.

Microsoft would later discover a long-forgotten bug that had originated in Win95 and remained in Windows for another 19 years. One developer came forward as the source of the bug, with the caveat that we would not give his name.

ANONYMOUS, *Software Engineer*:
It's like a Navajo rug, there's always a flaw built in. They say you have to leave one critical bug unpatched to allow any evil spirits in the software to escape. You know, developer angst, unfinished business, bad vibes.

SHERMAN SANDERS:
Yeah, that's what programmers tell themselves.

STEVE BALLMER:
I will neither confirm nor deny that this happens.

BILL GATES, *Former Chairman and CEO of Microsoft*:
Bullshit.

ANONYMOUS:
Look, it's not like it was going to do anything crazy. Other than allow someone to maliciously take over your computer. Look, we fixed it! Hurrah! Shut up.

May 1995. The Windows 95 team had slogged through feature development, tests and debugging, focus grouping, and the demands of marketing and PR. The release deadline was in sight. And then they were confronted by a final, unexpected foe: the Internet. For Bill Gates had discovered the World Wide Web.

BILL GATES, *Former Chairman and CEO of Microsoft*:
I was in my office practicing jumping over my desk chair. It's just something I do to get the blood pumping. I got bored and started playing around with Netscape. I went to Lycos to see if there was any kind of competitive chair-jumping circuit. I didn't find anything, but then I started looking at all of these awesome sites. Like HotWired, and the Real Audio Homepage. Crazy stuff. And there were no Microsoft files on any of them. I realized that we were missing out on the goddamn Information Superhighway. A superhighway that should have been bumper to bumper with .doc and Windows.exe files!

CAROLYN POMEROY, *Bill Gates' Assistant*:
Bill came out and asked me what I knew about the Internet. I showed him a homepage I made for Wexler, my cockatoo. Then he said, "Never mind," and told me to buy him a taller chair.

BILL GATES:
Wexler.com was just one of ten thousand websites out there. Ten thousand. This was the future. I sat down at my desk and started making a plan to conquer the Internet.

Bill Gates proceeded to write the infamous memo "The Internet Tidal Wave." This memo announced that Microsoft's primary focus would be integrating the Internet into all of their products and future strategy.

TODD BRONSTEIN, *VP, Microsoft Chicago*:
I always cringe when I see a big memo in my inbox. All edicts from above are announced that way. And the last thing you want is a major change of focus that affects the project you're working on. I read just the title and immediately headed out to the courtyard with my BMX.

LANCE JACKSON, *Software Engineer*:
Yeah, so Bill sends us this big memo about how we have to be all about the Internet. And Todd flipped out.

TODD BRONSTEIN:
We were past our final beta release. This was late May of 1995. We were releasing to manufacturing in August. We couldn't add Internet features in three months. This was catastrophic. I spent the next hour doing jumps onto a railing while simultaneously flipping off Bill's office. I sprained my wrist wiping out on the stairs.

VLAD MICHAEL MURRAY, *Software Engineer*:
Todd came back to his office looking pretty banged up. He started reading the memo. Then he went into the server room and shut the door. I could hear muffled screams. I headed for the pixy.

LANCE JACKSON:
You have to understand...the Internet was a giant pile of crap at that point. URLs were 900 characters long. People still had "Links" as a section on their websites. And they'd be linking to stuff like the U.S. Geological Survey. Websites still had counters on them. We were still looking as ASCII porn because it didn't take as long to load. Half of the pages on whitehouse.gov still had that picture of the guy with the shovel that said "This Page Is Under Construction."

See Figure.08 (page 79) for the White House website in 1995.

JOSH COOPER, *Software Engineer*:
E-commerce wasn't really a thing. I was still making arrangements to buy rare Magic: The Gathering cards via email and I had to pay for them with money orders.

TODD BRONSTEIN:
I tried to make it work. I ran the numbers again and again. But the schedule was too tight. There was no way to write a browser in three months.

BRIANNA LEE, *Software Development Manager*:
So Todd called an emergency meeting. He said, "Well, what have we got that's *like* the Internet?" Kanwar said, "MSN."

KANWAR KHAN, *Software Engineer*:
I said, "MSN." It got really quiet. Todd started to cry.

LISA K., *Software Engineer*:
No, I said, "MSN." I said, "MSN," like 5 times but nobody heard me! Sexist fuckwads.

STAN BANAS, *Software Engineer*:
I mean, who wouldn't cry? MSN was Microsoft's attempt to make our own AOL, because the world *totally* needed another AOL. *Anyone* could tell you that people would line up to pay a monthly fee so they could tie up their phone line to look at a stripped-down version of America Online's "Court TV Law Center." Or open several folders in order to find today's weather. Even CompuServe had a web browser by then. Fucking CompuServe was on the bleeding edge, compared to us!

MARC ANDREESSEN, *Co-Founder, Netscape*:
I laughed my ass off the first time I saw MSN. I subscribed to MSN just so I could laugh at it. It really cheered me up whenever I was having a bad day. It was better than Prozac.

See Figure.09 (page 80) for the home screen of The Microsoft Network.

As the launch approached, the team went into a frenzy. Compromises were made. Battle lines were drawn, redrawn, crossed out again, and forgotten due to lack of sleep.

LISA K.:
We were so tired. Some people couldn't even remember how to get to their own offices. They just circled through the building and circled and circled until they became exhausted and passed out in the hallway.

LANCE JACKSON:
I tried to keep it light. Whenever anyone came into my office I'd say "Welcome to Windows 96!"

KANWAR KHAN:
Yes. Lance made that joke repeatedly. Until Calvin went off on him.
He called him a pretentious, oversharing, shit-coding, Vanpool Nazi
asshat and asked him if he knew the origin of the word "asshat." You
could hear it all the way across the building. It went on for like 30
minutes.

JOSH COOPER:
That was pretty satisfying.

CALVIN VASQUEZ, *Software Engineer*:
Yes. Oh yes.

LANCE JACKSON:
I was floored. It just came out of nowhere. He quit the vanpool for
three weeks. He took the bus!

VLAD MICHAEL MURRAY:
It was tense. I remember we all got pretty bitter when we found out
that Stan Banas got Level 13 for what seemed like no reason. So right
before he got his card for the vending machines, we bought all the
good stuff out of every machine on the floor, just to spite him. There
was nothing left but corn nuts and gum.

STAN BANAS:
It ruined what was supposed to be the best day of my life.

BRIANNA LEE:
Crunch time is the worst. My daughter was five at the time. I
remember bringing her to work with me on weekends. Microsoft
said there'd be temporary daycare but I think they just let them run
around in Cairo's old area.

EUNICE LEE, *Former Child*:
It was wild. All the kids were amped up on soda and candy. I wasn't
allowed to drink soda, but it was all over the place, so they couldn't
really stop me.

TYLER UNTERBERG, *Former Child*:
Eunice Lee was just brutal. One of my earliest childhood memories
was getting hit in the eye when she threw a nerf football at my face.

DANNY HÖFFLER, *Former Child:*
I used to draw pictures on the whiteboards. My dad wanted me to
play with Microsoft Bob, but it just made me sad.

TYLER UNTERBERG:
We used to play "kick me out of the meeting." We sat in chairs in a circle
and one person was Bill Gates. Then you'd get up and walk around
like in musical chairs and when the music stopped, whoever ended up
sitting across from Bill Gates would get kicked out of the meeting.

EUNICE LEE:
I was *always* Bill Gates.

LANCE JACKSON:
Pixy use got out of control. Everyone was using except Banas. Nerd.
One night we found Vlad in the break room with the acute smell of
burnt sugar in the air. He'd tried to caramelize. It was bad. Acute
sucrose toxicity. He was in the hospital for 17 days.

VLAD MICHAEL MURRAY:
I missed the last two weeks before delivery. And I'm never going to
forgive myself for that. Fucking pixy.

TODD BRONSTEIN:
It was a turning point for the group. When we nearly lost Vlad, we
all had to take a moment to reflect. It made us want to focus only on
the important things in life. Like delivering Windows 95 on time.

But Windows 95 still had no Internet capabilities.

TODD BRONSTEIN:
We were out of ideas. My bike was in the shop. I headed over to
Building 8 to throw myself on the mercy of Bill. By the time I got
there, he'd already solved it.

BILL GATES:
I had an epiphany. I was playing 3D Pinball and I thought: We're
Microsoft. Let's just license another company's browser, rename it,
and stick it in a fifty dollar upgrade. Done!

JOSH COOPER:
And that's the story of Internet Explorer 1.0.

KANWAR KHAN:
(singing) *All Hail Bill Gates / For He Hath Solv-ed The Internet For Ever and Ever!*

BRIANNA LEE:
But it was still too late to integrate it into Win95, so we just put MSN in and hoped nobody would open it.

TODD BRONSTEIN:
Bill was right about the Internet, of course. Netscape had its IPO 15 days before we launched, and then it really was all about the Web. It would have been hella awesome if he'd been right earlier.

After 3 years of work, 950 builds, 6000 bugs, 8.5 tons of pixy, 7.4 billion gallons of soda and 5 casualties, Windows 95 was ready to release.

TODD BRONSTEIN:
It went the way it always does. Eventually, the hard work pays off. You squash the bugs, you run the tests, you meet the quality standard and you're done.

BRIANNA LEE:
It went the way it always does. At a certain point we ran out of time, said, "Good enough!" then pushed it out the door and went to Denny's. End of story.

We traveled to California to visit Larry Belder, author of Windows 95 for Dummies and his wife Marilyn Fortson Belder, author of the Complete Idiot's Guide to Windows 95.

LARRY BELDER, *Author*:
We met at a convention for writers for Dummies. I had written *Shareware for Canadians for Dummies* and she had written *Installing Your Printer for Seniors for Dummies*.

MARILYN FORTSON BELDER, *Author*:
I was standing outside a meeting room at the San Jose Hilton, waiting to go in for a panel called "Special Topics in Bulleted Lists."

LARRY BELDER:
I saw her wearing a button that said "Ask Me About My Lactose Intolerance" and it made me laugh and I introduced myself. After the panel, I bought her a soy latte and we talked for hours.

MARILYN FORTSON BELDER:
I actually do have lactose intolerance, and all my conversations end up there anyway. Having a button just cuts to the chase. Larry had given up dairy for ethical reasons. So we had that and For Dummies in common. A year later we were married.

LARRY BELDER:
We had a little study at home with desks that faced each other and we'd pitch lists back and forth. It was a great couple of years. But then we both tried to get the Windows 95 contract and they hired me. And she went over to the dark side.

MARILYN FORTSON BELDER:
I'd heard that the Idiots were looking for someone and I thought...
well, I can be a second string peripherals writer or leave and
move up.

LARRY BELDER:
Leaving the Dummies family is a big deal. People just don't do it.
Once you're in, you're in for life.

MARILYN FORTSON BELDER:
I think he looked at it as a personal betrayal. But this is popular
instructional manual creation. It's not about loyalty, it's about sales.

LARRY BELDER:
I said, "Baby, I love you. We'll make it work." But in order to avoid a
conflict of interest, we had to completely separate our processes.

MARILYN FORTSON BELDER:
It was crazy. We built a wall of bookcases splitting the study in
half. We sat in silence during meals and then went back to our
halves. Eventually, the strain on our marriage was too much and I
moved out.

LARRY BELDER:
We separated for a year. The books came out. Both huge hits. But it
wasn't enough.

MARILYN FORTSON BELDER:
I was miserable. He was miserable. There had to be another solution.
So we took our Idiots and Dummies money and bought an almond
orchard in Bakersfield. I write on the porch and he writes in the barn.
We don't talk shop after 6pm. And it's been 20 years.

LARRY BELDER:
That experience tested us, but it turned out our marriage was
stronger than Windows 95.

MARILYN FORTSON BELDER:
We found out our true priorities. Family first, then Idiots and Dummies.

LARRY BELDER:
I'd like to clear up one thing: Dummies books are not for actual
Dummies. They're for people who don't have time to be experts.

MARILYN FORTSON BELDER:
The Idiot's books *are* aimed at idiots. They're much harder to write.

LARRY BELDER:
Our son David left home to work for O'Reilly. (Sighs) We never see him.

Marilyn and Larry Belder weren't the only writers attached to Windows 95. We visited the basement offices of freelance email joke writers Gordon Stanley and Terry Pyler.

GORDON STANLEY, *Jokesmith*:
We'd been ghostwriting rec.arts.funny on Usenet for a couple years at that point and then decided to get into email forwards. Terry and I met when we both had competing sets of 100 Blonde Jokes. We decided to team up and we've been writing together ever since.

TERRY PYLER, *Jokesmith*:
So the jokes have to come out before release. That's the expectation. But it's not like you have a beta or anything. You start by generalizing from the name, and from the general perception of Microsoft. "Why is it called Windows 95? Because it installs on 95 floppy discs." That joke writes itself. Others take a little more time.

GORDON STANLEY:
Bill Gates – it's never not funny to mention Bill Gates. How many Windows 95s does it take to screw in a lightbulb…actually that one didn't work.

TERRY PYLER:
A week before launch we stayed up all night, pitching jokes until we had 10K. Then forward, forward, forward.

GORDON STANLEY:
The response was amazing. My uncle Marty forwarded it back to me within days.

RONALD SVARZBEIN, *Admin, rec.arts.funny*:
Yeah, I remember that one. I mean, something about Windows 95 is never going to have the staying power of 100 Blonde Jokes, but for topical material, it was a monster.

GORDON STANLEY:
We became legend. We were the highest paid ghostwriters rec.arts. funny ever employed.

RONALD SVARZBEIN:
We don't employ writers. Who said that?

TERRY PYLER:
We were pros back then. You might say we were in the first wave of internet content creation.

GORDON STANLEY:
It's a real skill to write an uncredited joke. It's like Tin Pan Alley, writing all those standards, just riffing away in obscurity.

RONALD SVARZBEIN:
But the Gershwins were credited.

GORDON STANLEY:
Just riffing away…

BILL GATES, *Former Chairman and CEO of Microsoft*:
I banned the IP of rec.arts.funny before launch. We were under enough pressure. Also, those guys are assholes.

Hundreds of people waited in line for the software's midnight release. Some chain stores offered free pizza and other perks.

JEROME CRAIG, *Security Guard*:
I mean, we had serious, rock-star level security at CompUSA. We were expecting a mob. And we got one. We haven't had that big of a rush since SimLife. Or Civilization 1.

RALPH BOYLER, *Windows Devotee*:
I had a buddy who worked at CompUSA in New Brunswick and he told me there would be free pizza if we lined up for the release at midnight, so I got in line at 7pm. I remember purposely depriving myself of pizza that day, knowing that free pizza was the sweetest of pizzas. It was a long wait. I brought *Snow Crash* to read. The guy in front of me kept talking about something called the Task Bar. This was before you could pretend to stare at your phone. I remember that after a couple of hours a bunch of teens started to sing. They kept singing "Cotton Eye Joe" over and over again and after a while everyone was doing it. Nerds. I had that stuck in my head for days.

JEROME CRAIG:
I remember this one guy getting in my face about cutting the line.

BRYCE JOHNSON, *Windows Devotee:*
I thought people who were members of the CompUSA Premium club would get preferential line positions. Clearly, that was not the case.

JEROME CRAIG:
Yeah, I don't know what that was about.

JAN SZLAGA, *Former Head of Marketing for CompUSA:*
There is not now and has never been a CompUSA premium club. Who said that? Sorry, I have to go. I have a group interview at Fry's.

JOEL X., *Windows Protester:*
I've protested at every Windows software release, but that was the biggest. It was insane. There were like 200 people in line already when I showed up with my sign that said "del windows.sux." One guy said that if I had Windows 95 I could say "Windows 95 Sucks. exe." I punched him in the face.

RALPH BOYLER:
I saw that guy! That's what stopped the singing. He punched a guy in the face and got tazed. I thought it was because of the singing. Luckily, that was after I'd gotten to the pizza. Sweet, sweet pizza.

JEROME CRAIG:
I think some people didn't even buy a copy of Windows 95. Freeloading weirdos.

RALPH BOYLER:
I bought it. Yeah, I figured, what the hell. It was pretty expensive though. $89 in 1995 dollars, if you can believe that. Which is like… (he does a lookup and a quick calculation on his iPad) slightly more than Windows 8 cost. Oh. Can you watch my iPad for a sec? I'm going to get a banana.

JOEL X.:
I maintain that graphical user interfaces are for the weak-minded and imagination-impaired. Windows was, and continues to be, an abomination. I'm still using DOS. I can't get into Linux. Who am I, Helen Hunt? ✖

8/24/95. Launch day. It took a 200-person crew 20 days to prepare the Microsoft Campus for the legendary Windows 95 launch event. Jay Leno of The Tonight Show hosted. At the end, there was a special appearance by the Windows 95 development team.

TODD BRONSTEIN, *VP, Microsoft Chicago*:
We told everyone to wear their nicest khakis. It was going to be wall to wall press and we wanted everyone's appearance to reflect well on Microsoft. That was a big ask for some people. You're lucky if you can get developers to wear shoes.

LANCE JACKSON, *Software Engineer*:
I thought my ex-girlfriend might see me on TV, so I wore the sexy Dockers.

VLAD MICHAEL MURRAY, *Software Engineer*:
When we got to work they threw t-shirts at us and told us to wait outside the big tent. They were going to drop a curtain at the end of the presentation and show everyone who worked on 95 standing on bleachers, wearing shirts that made the Microsoft logo. And then the press would walk between the bleachers and listen to us cheer like a pep rally.

STAN BANAS, *Software Engineer*:
I did not get into software so that I could attend pep rallies. And they wanted the left side to yell "Windows!" and the right side to yell "95!" Lame. So I started a bunch of cheers like "Marco!" "Polo!" "Disco!" "Inferno!" and "Cheering!" "Sucks!"

BRIANNA LEE, *Software Development Manager*:
Stan was particularly not into it, because his wife asked for a divorce during the last week of crunch time. Oh yeah, Stan Banas was married. We didn't even know that until he got divorced.

LANCE JACKSON:
Yeah, for a guy who complains that much, the fact that he never mentioned her at all was a shocker.

STAN BANAS:
I didn't wear a ring. I have sensitive skin. None of this is your business.

LISA K., *Software Engineer*:
Then there was a kerfuffle because nobody wanted to stand in the yellow section.

TODD BRONSTEIN:
How many project managers does it take to get a Microsoftie to wear a stupid t-shirt and cheer one word? Twenty-seven. It's not a joke.

JOSH COOPER, *Software Engineer*:
Finally they negotiated free beer for just that section. Which was awesome, because it was 10am. Woo! Yellow section!

DEREK UNTERBERG, *VP, Microsoft Cairo*:
I was in charge of crowd control. Bill was still pissed at me for Cairo.

KANWAR KHAN, *Software Engineer*:
I wasn't on the bleachers. I was performing with the Microsoft Chorus during the festivities. We sang a show choir version of "Start Me Up" before Jay Leno walked onstage.

BILL GATES, *Former Chairman and CEO of Microsoft*:
Melinda had written a little comedy sketch for me to do with Jay Leno. Jay would pretend that he didn't understand computers and then I would say, "Jay, it looks like you don't understand computers" and then Jay would show *me* how to use Windows 95 and he'd be correct. Ha!

BRIANNA LEE:
I heard about that. It was genius, like something the Harvard Lampoon would come up with.

MELINDA GATES, *Comedy Enthusiast:*
I was pretty proud of that. But then again, I knew Jay. I'd been faxing jokes into *The Tonight Show* for years.

JAY LENO:
I brought my writers, because we needed to make sure we had monologue jokes that were tailored to the Windows 95 launch. My writers determined that the most appropriate course was to do all the old OJ Simpson and Ross Perot stuff and just add "Windows 95" and "Bill Gates" to them. It destroyed.

KARL SHINKMAN, *Fatal Exception Manager:*
I was in the audience. I snuck in just in case the demo crashed. When the Blue Screen of Death came up, I was going to yell, "That was me!" It didn't crash. I was bummed.

MICKI DAVIDSON, *Windows Groupie:*
Jessica and I were really worried they wouldn't take our fake IDs but we totally got in. We missed the demo, but outside there was, like, a circus. There were tents with software demos and stuff. There was a booth where you could get your face morphed with Bill Gates to see what your future children would look like.

JESSICA SKRONA, *Windows Groupie:*
You could sign up for a free month of MSN. It was, like, my dream. Plus there was a Ferris wheel. And a hot air balloon!

MICKI DAVIDSON:
Free soda and hot dogs! Swag! I got a ton of mousepads!

JESSICA SKRONA:
And Flea was there. I got to go up in a hot air balloon with Flea! He signed my boob.

MICKI DAVIDSON:
They totally made out.

JESSICA SKRONA:
I got his signature tattooed over when we got back to Portland. But I had it removed when I turned 30.

MICKI DAVIDSON:
I got 13 floppy discs inked down my arm. It's a full installation sleeve. I feel like that one's aged a little better.

ERIN HOLLAND, *Event Planner*:
Flea was the only celebrity who showed for the party. We tried to
get a band to play, but the Rolling Stones were touring, Brian Eno
had the flu, and Weezer was recording Pinkerton. And you can't just
have Flea playing.

FLEA, *Bassist, The Red Hot Chili Peppers*:
I offered, but they said that would be weird. So I just hung out in the
hot air balloon and made out with chicks.

SHARON DAVIS, *Public Relations Legend*:
I did everything I could to persuade them, but Matthew Perry and
Jennifer Aniston wouldn't come to the afterparty. They are dead to me.

ERIN HOLLAND, *Event Planner*:
We ended up showing the Buddy Holly video on a loop and just
hiring a DJ.

EDIE BRICKELL, *Musician*
Nobody even invited me. My video was in the Plus Pack! Good Times!

VLAD MICHAEL MURRAY:
The afterparty was nuts. I mean, free soda, whatever, but then they
brought the booze out. They had an actual bar called The Task Bar.
Where the task was...getting obliterated, I guess. People left to hook
up. I think all the Word people fucked all the Excel people. I mean, we
all knew that was going to happen sometime. The tension between
those groups was palpable.

BURT GWAR, *Cairo Developer*:
I got really drunk and I got on Derek's case about the fact that Cairo
never shipped. I reminded him he said he'd jump off a bridge. He said
he'd dive into Lake Bill if it would shut me up. So we walked down to
the lake.

BRIANNA LEE:
The bigwigs went to Bill Gates's mansion to get super high and watch
all the art change on all the video screens. I hear that's where the word
Zune came from. They were too baked to say they were zoning out. Or
someone was Dutch, I don't know.

VLAD MICHAEL MURRAY:
It got out of control. People started to do pixy in the bathrooms. I
called my sponsor.

STAN BANAS:
Yeah, Vlad called me and we got out of there.

BRIANNA LEE:
We decided to go to Lake Bill and hang out.

LISA K.:
I think I needed to process that it was really over.

JOSH COOPER:
We sat on a rock and talked for a long time. We knew the group was splitting up. I'd already been assigned to NT 3.5. Lance and Vlad were staying on to do some service pack updates. Calvin was going to a startup. Brianna Lee and Stan Banas were cashing out and retiring. Kanwar was on sabbatical until the Microsoft Chorus finished its three year world tour. Lisa K...I forget.

LISA K.:
I was going on maternity leave! I was 8 ½ months pregnant. Did everyone forget that? Jesus.

LANCE JACKSON:
I think it was Calvin's idea to push the van into Lake Bill. It seemed like a great idea at the time.

CALVIN VASQUEZ, *Software Engineer:*
Heh.

VLAD MICHAEL MURRAY:
He wanted us to set it on fire and give it a Viking funeral, but we talked him down to just pushing it into the lake.

BRIANNA LEE:
We got it out of the parking garage. Then we had to put it in neutral, push it between the buildings, then up and over a hill. Luckily security was pretty occupied with the party. I heard something about Flea being missing. Then Todd showed up.

TODD BRONSTEIN:
I was pretty wasted. I tried to jump onto the roof of the van on my bike. That's how I got this scar.

LISA K.:
I felt bad. He scared the koi.

KANWAR KHAN:
That weirdo Burt who used to be on Cairo showed up with Derek Unterberg, but when they saw Todd wipe out they just turned around and left. Derek hooked up with a Dockers model that night. They're married now.

BURT GWAR:
Todd Bronstein did some insane stunt and wiped out in Lake Bill. I thought I was hallucinating, so I went back to the office to sleep it off. Just for the hell of it, I opened the time machine program and started messing with it. And suddenly, it started up. It said, "Where Do You Want to Go Today?" And I said, "Take me back to before Windows 95 so I can get my life back." And then it froze. I rebooted it four times and then I just deleted it.

LANCE JACKSON:
The rental place would not let us get another van. So we all bought Miatas. And the Vanpool 8 went our separate ways.

JOSH COOPER:
It was true, the people who stayed got windows. I got two windows.

BRIANNA LEE:
I retired and the first thing I did was build myself a greenhouse.

LANCE JACKSON:
I did get a window, but I didn't get my girlfriend back. Now that I think about it, she dumped me for working late all the time, so working late to get a window to impress her didn't make a lot of sense. Oh well. I like the view.

KAYLIE MANCINI, *Windows Enthusiast:*
I love Windows 95. I still run it. It's so old that it won't run most modern viruses. And it's very fast on my homemade PC. I also love Word 3.1.

TODD BRONSTEIN:
I've told my grandchildren that I worked on 95. I made them bring the box to show and tell. Apparently the discussion was short. It's 3rd grade. When they get older, they'll understand why I'm a hero.

BILL GATES:
We've spent an awfully long time talking about Windows 95. Do you *have* any questions about Windows 10 or are you just wasting my time? ×

EPILOGUE

Microsoft sold over 40 million copies of Windows 95 in its first year of release.

The Windows 95 team was awarded the Pulitzer Prize for Special Achievement in Garnering Journalistic Coverage.

Bill Clinton presented Windows 95 with the Presidential Medal of Freedom.

Windows 95 was adapted into a TV series on Canadian television, which ran for one season. It starred Colm Feore as the Start Menu, Maury Chaykin as the Recycle Bin, and Sarah Polley as Windows Explorer.

After Windows 98 was released, Windows 95 was commemorated in the *In Memoriam* segment of the Oscars.

In 2015, a cache of untouched copies of Windows 95 were found in a landfill in Bellevue, Washington. They were sold at Christie's to a private collector for $250,000. When opened, they turned out to be mis-labeled copies of Microsoft Bob. They were then re-buried.

IT'S NOW SAFE TO SHUT DOWN YOUR COMPUTER.

FIGURES

FIGURE.01

The usability group's report on the graphical user interface for Windows 3.1

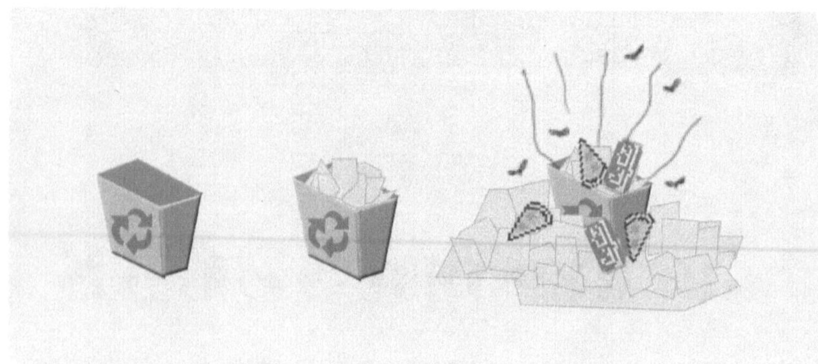

The Chicago team originally conceived the Recycle Bin with an empty state, a full state and an overflowing state. Users would be expected to sort through their files periodically or the bin would become filled with of garbage, attract flies and crash. This idea survived through 201 builds before it was deemed "gross."

FIGURE.03

Early version of the Start Button, aimed at extremely stupid users.

FIGURE.04

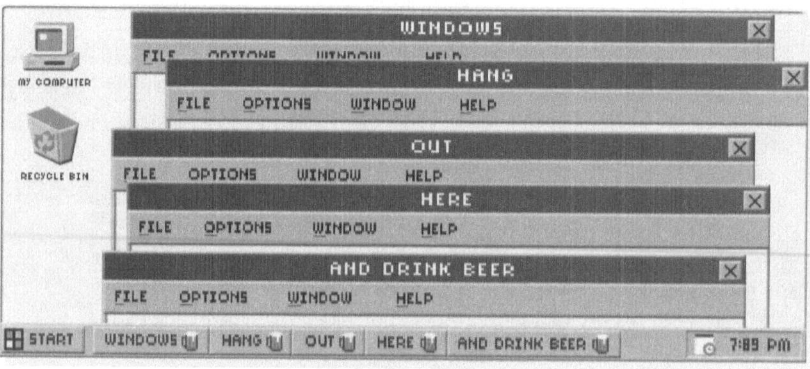

Early concept illustration of the Windows Taskbar.

FIGURE.05

WINDOWS

DON'T FREAK OUT, BUT AN ERROR HAS OCCURRED.

MAKE YOURSELF SOME TEA AND TAKE ALL THE TIME YOU NEED TO WRITE THIS DOWN.

THIS HAPPENS ALL THE TIME. HUMANS AND MACHINES ARE FALLIBLE. IT MAY BE POSSIBLE TO CONTINUE NORMALLY. HOW ABOUT WE TRY THIS:

*YOU CAN PRESS ANY KEY TO ATTEMPT TO CONTINUE. MAYBE IT'S NOTHING.

*PRESS CTRL+ALT+DELETE TO RESTART YOUR COMPUTER. UNFORTUNATELY, YOU WILL LOSE ANY UNSAVED INFORMATION IN ALL APPLICATIONS. BUT IT'S OKAY. IT'S JUST WORK. YOU ARE MORE THAN YOUR UNSAVED INFORMATION. YOU WILL BE FINE. MORE THAN FINE.

BREATHE.

WINDOWS

*****FATAL ERROR*****FATAL ERROR*****
*****FATAL ERROR*****FATAL ERROR*****

WHAT DID YOU DO?

A *****FATAL ERROR***** HAS OCCURRED.

STOP WHAT YOU ARE DOING AND WRITE THIS DOWN OR ELSE!

IT MAY BE POSSIBLE TO CONTINUE NORMALLY, IF YOU LIVE IN A FANTASY WORLD.

*YOU CAN PRESS ANY KEY TO ATTEMPT TO CONTINUE, BUT LET'S GET REAL - YOU'RE HOSED. BUT IF YOU'RE SOME KIND OF POLLYANNA, GO AHEAD, KNOCK YOURSELF OUT.

*PRESS CTRL+ALT+DELETE TO RESTART YOUR COMPUTER. YOU WILL LOSE ANY UNSAVED INFORMATION IN ALL APPLICATIONS. BUT YOU WERE SMART ENOUGH TO SAVE YOUR WORK, NOT! HOPE IT WASN'T IMPORTANT.

THIS IS ALL YOUR FAULT. I HOPE YOU LEARNED SOMETHING.

Two early drafts of the Blue Screen of Death.

Microsoft Bob. People actually bought this.

```c
#include <stdio.h>
/*
* * * * * * * * * * * * * * * * * * * * * * * * * * * * *
* So Much Depends (After WCW)                          *
*                   by Xander Howells                  *
*                                                      *
*    so much depends                                   *
*    upon                                              *
*    Marvin                                            *
*    having any ability                                *
*    to code                                           *
*    you stole my fruitopia                            *
*    you dick                                          *
*                                                      *
* * * * * * * * * * * * * * * * * * * * * * * * * * * * *


XH:
.........................../´¯/)
.........................,/¯../
......................../.../
..................../´¯/'...'/´¯¯`·
................../'/.../..../......./¨¯\
.................('(...´...´.... ¯~/'...')
..................\.................'...../
...................''...\.......... _.·´
.....................\..............(
.......................\.............\...
 - MB


* * * * * * * * * * * * * * * * * * * * * * * * * * * * *
*                                                      *
*    you                                               *
*    and your soul patch                               *
*    can eat me                                        *
*                   - XH                               *
*                                                      *
* * * * * * * * * * * * * * * * * * * * * * * * * * * * *
*/


int main(void){
```

Microsoft Cairo's ongoing code comment war.

The White House homepage in 1995.

FIGURE.09

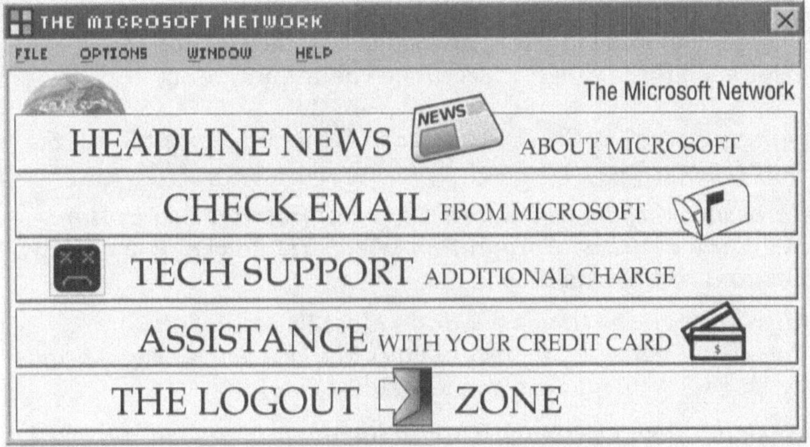

Microsoft's portal to the Internet.

AFTERWORD

Special thanks to Sarah Boyer, Dan Eder, Michael Gerber, Dax Herrera, Mike Levine, Haley Mancini, George Oz, Dawn Wells, and the Devastator staff (Meredith Donahue, John Ford, Micki Grover, Lee Keeler, and Kenny Keil) for reading early drafts, answering technical questions and listening to my book madness. And to my editors Geoffrey Golden and Amanda Meadows for their encouragement and patience throughout this ridiculously complex project. Extra special thanks to my Contributing Editors Patrick Baker and Asterios Kokkinos for helping unstick the really difficult parts, and adding many, many funny jokes. I owe all of you snacks.

Various books and articles provided factual information and inspiration for this highly inaccurate volume, including:

Showstopper!: The Breakneck Race to Create Windows NT and the Next Generation at Microsoft by G. Pascal Zachary

Barbarians Led by Bill Gates: Microsoft from the Inside: How the World's Richest Corporation Wields Its Power by Jennifer Edstrom and Marlin Eller

Microsoft Secrets: How the World's Most Powerful Software Company Creates Technology, Shapes Markets and Manages People by Michael A. Cusumano and Richard W. Selby

I Sing the Body Electronic: A Year with Microsoft on the Multimedia Frontier by Fred Moody

Dreaming in Code: Two Dozen Programmers, Three Years, 4,732 Bugs, and One Quest for Transcendent Software by Scott Rosenberg

Microserfs: A Novel by Douglas Coupland

I Want My MTV: The Uncensored Story of the Music Video Revolution by Rob Tannenbaum and Craig Marks

"The Internet Tidal Wave" by Bill Gates

This book was written in Microsoft Word 2004 on a very old MacBook Pro.

ABOUT THE AUTHOR

Lesley Tsina is comedy writer and actor who has appeared on *Community*, *Black-ish*, *Funny or Die Presents* and was Contributing Editor for cult humor anthology series *The Devastator*. She is a former technical writer, so her last book was a pile of documentation about cell phone ringtones which the *New York Times* described as "gripping." She performs at the Upright Citizens Brigade Theatre and tours with a one-woman show about being laid off from a tech company, *Lord of the Files*. She is originally from Palo Alto, CA, and it shows.